Jake Poller was born i̱ ..ves and works in London. *Reach* is his first novel.

REACH

JAKE POLLER

Jonathan Cape
London

Published by Jonathan Cape 1999

2 4 6 8 10 9 7 5 3 1

First published in Great Britain in 1999 by
Jonathan Cape
Random House, 20 Vauxhall Bridge Road, London SW1V 2SA

Random House Australia (Pty) Limited
20 Alfred Street, Milsons Point, Sydney,
New South Wales 2061, Australia

Random House New Zealand Limited
18 Poland Road, Glenfield,
Auckland 10, New Zealand

Random House South Africa (Pty) Limited
Endulini, 5A Jubilee Road, Parktown 2193, South Africa

Random House UK Limited Reg. No. 954009

A CIP catalogue record for this book
is available from the British Library

ISBN 0–224–05296–9

Papers used by Random House UK Limited are natural,
recyclable products made from wood grown in sustainable forests.
The manufacturing processes conform to the environmental
regulations of the country of origin.

Typeset by Deltatype Ltd, Birkenhead, Merseyside
Printed and bound in Great Britain by
Creative Print and Design (Wales), Ebbw Vale

For my mother and father

1

'But what's he doing?' asks Anthony.

'What's he doing? He's having a wank.'

'But how d'you know that? It doesn't *say* he's having a wank.'

Anthony, who regards the subtle and elliptical as wilful stratagems on the part of the author to make him appear dim, is referring to 'An Encounter' by James Joyce.

'Look, first the old "josser", as Joyce has it, is talking about tottie. Then when he comes back he's talking about whipping naughty boys, and how much naughty boys actively *need* to be whipped, and how he'd just *die* to give them all a good birching!'

Anthony is clearly unconvinced by my explication.

'Personally, I'm all for it,' I say, lighting a cigarette.

'What?'

'Birching.'

'What's that?'

'It's when you spank unruly boys' *bums* with a birch branch.'

'Oh.' Then, as the unspeakable idea dawns on him: 'You're not, um … *gay*, are you?'

'And if I were?' Sensing that Anthony is about to make a break for it, I assure him: 'No. I'm not.'

For the past two months I have been trying to instil in Anthony, if not a passion, then at least a liking, for English literature. Progress has been slow. My pupil, you see, prefers the sciences – has, to my mind, an unhealthy attachment to the concrete and unequivocal. The laws of physics. Logic. Scientific 'truth'. Hard to believe, then, that his father, a fellow of St John's College, Cambridge, taught me everything I know about Kyd's *The Spanish Tragedy*. When his parents separated, six months ago, he and his mother came to live in the maisonette at the top of my grandmother's house on the Old Brompton Road. Hitherto, Anthony had attended a spartan boarding school just outside Cambridge – which, far from making him a man, patently retarded his emotional development. He is now a pupil at Latymer, a second-rate public school in Hammersmith, where, as far as I can tell, he is only marginally less miserable. But then again misery is the very stuff of adolescence – an emotion uniquely and unhappily suited to boys of sixteen.

We first met when I moved in with my grandmother back in January. And, upon learning that he was having difficulties with his A-level English, I offered to help – as, having been taught for so long, I was avid to teach. Anthony proved to be a spiky pupil, and, such was his initial resentment and scorn, I suggested he drop the subject. But when it transpired that he'd only taken English out of fealty to his father, I took pity: If only, I thought, we'd each been sired by the other's dad, we could've made them proud; for I sensed that Anthony would get on with my father – a professor of mathematics at UCL – far better than I ever had; and for a time up at Cambridge I'd been Dr Fowler's protégé – until, that is, apoplectic on pink gin, he made a pass at me.

'D'you have a girlfriend?'

'No.'

'Neither do I. Of course if I wanted one . . .'

'Hey. Me too,' I say, suppressing a smile.

'I mean, girls. Godolphin girls, anyway. They're . . . they're all so pretentious.'

And, looking at Anthony, at his thin fair hair, his boyish bumfluff, at the spots that bespatter his forehead, and, less densely, his chin, I can well imagine the repugnance he excites in haughty schoolgirls, the frustration he feels, for at his age I was equally charmless.

Then, wistfully: 'If only I had a car . . .'

'Anyway. You'd better go. I've got to go to work.'

'An MG'd be nice,' he says dreamily.

Standing up, I say: 'You can't even drive.' And, opening the door: 'I'll see you Sunday.'

'Sunday?' Then, shucking off his reverie: 'Oh, yes. Sunday. See you then.'

2

I have been working part-time (every other evening) at a bookshop, wittily called The Book Shop, for the past six weeks. At first I was somewhat peeved that my colleagues instantly surmised that I'd been to Cambridge and that this was my first job – primarily because I *was* at Cambridge and this *is* (notwithstanding a brief stint as a paperboy) my first job. And because, up at Cambridge, I'd always thought of myself as different – even unique – neither a beblazered rugger-bugger nor a dope-addled anarchist manqué. Before I started I'd absurdly presupposed that my fellow booksellers and I would be locking antlers over Pynchon, Beckett and Joyce – when, in actuality, the most heated discussions are about *The Simpsons* and *Wallace and Grommet*. Which isn't to say that The Book Shop doesn't have its share of would-be poets, playwrights and painters; on the contrary, my part-time colleagues all regard themselves as artists of some stamp: Victoria is a poetess; Kay – the only published member of staff – writes children's books; Steve, whose ever-burgeoning 1000-page novel, *The Death of Love*, has been rejected some forty-three times, is either a charlatan or a genius (I say ever-burgeoning because every time it's rejected he tacks on an epilogue in which the offending editor is either maimed or murdered by the volatile narrator – author and unsung hero of the unpublished 1000-page masterpiece, *The Death of Love*); Clare is a photographer; Iseult, a painter; Phil, an art student at Central St Martin's; and Judy, while not strictly speaking an artist, has none the less been writing an epic doctoral thesis on George Eliot for the past ten years; even Rez, the store detective, is writing a screenplay – *Don't Fuck With Me, Nigger* – about an undercover cop who infiltrates an LA gang, crosses the line, loses the edge, and, in a tragic denouement, is killed by his ex-partner in a heist. As for myself, after coming down from Cambridge, I signed on the dole and spent the next six months trying to write a novel – which, just before Christmas, I locked in a drawer and haven't looked at since. In retrospect, I think I lacked the radical originality that bespeaks true talent; and try as I might to find a voice that was distinctly and inimitably my own, I always ended up sounding like a pallid imitation of somebody else – like Fowles, like Auster, like Roth. And whilst, I suppose, I still think of myself as a writer, my self-belief, once so hardy and impregnable, is at its lowest ebb.

3

Entering the staffroom, a windowless whitewashed cavern with crumbling plaster walls, I am greeted by Victoria. Each time I see her I am shocked anew by her appalling emaciation, for while she hides her body beneath shapeless baggy clothes – chunky cable jumpers and schoolmarmish ankle-length skirts – her head appears outsized on her spindly neck, and her hands are so frail and skeletal one fears they will snap as she struggles with an atlas, takes the strain of a dictionary; even ordinarily undemanding exertions – such as walking upstairs – leave her breathless and pale.

'I've brought a poem to show you,' she says, rummaging in her satchel.

'Oh, good,' I say, feigning enthusiasm, for her poems tend to read like the earnest outpourings of a precocious twelve-year-old.

She hands me a sheet of paper, at the top of which, as is her habit, she has printed her name and address.

I read the title out loud: '"Aestival Crepuscule".'

'It's rather Keatsian, don't you think?'

'I . . . see what you mean,' I say, steeling myself for the first stanza.

> O Helios! Thy Chariot speeds West,
> This Mortal Coil, darkling at Thy behest –
> Yonder, the Hesperides' Golden Tree
> Once plunderèd by Zeus's Progeny.
> Soon wilt Thou be borne back on Oceans' Stream
> And pitchy Night Thy Eastern Light redeem.

'What's that,' says Steve, craning over my shoulder.

'It's a sestina,' says Victoria defensively.

'Who the fuck writes *sestinas* nowadays?'

'*I* do.'

'It *is* a somewhat antiquated form,' I say, having given up on the second stanza.

'So what if it is?'

'I mean, Christ. You might as well try your hand at hieroglyphics.'

'Well, we can't all write "post-postmodern" novels, can we, Steve?'

'What makes it *post*-postmodern?' I ask.

'Trade secret,' he says enigmatically. Then: 'Oh, okay. Basically, the whole thing works on a metatextual level. In the prologue Derrida writes me this letter in which he deconstructs the novel. Basically, the whole novel is a reconstruct of Derrida's deconstruct. Then there's this dream sequence in which Foucault comes along and deconstructs *Derrida's* deconstruct. Then, inside *that* dream, there's this other dream in which *Lacan* –'

'He thinks he's a genius,' says Victoria derisively.

'I *am* a genius.'

'Then why haven't you been published?'

'As sure a sign as any.' Then, to me: 'Hey, Miff. Logodaedaly.'

'Not bad,' I say. 'Anfractuosity.'

'Oh, that's good.'

Steve and I have somehow fallen into the habit of hurling abstruse, preferably polysyllabic, words at each other.

'Keats was published. Shelley was published. Byron –'

'Yeah yeah yeah,' says Steve.

Just then there is a sickening thud. 'Blast!' says Judy, who, having somehow stubbed her toe, hops into the room. '*Ooh*' – her customary complaint – 'it's been one of those days.'

What to say about Judy? Where to begin? For a start, she is the most accident-prone person I've ever met – it's as if she hulks around with her an invisible tail, over which she is forever tripping up. In keeping with this corporeal clumsiness, her voice is every bit as quavery and erratic as a bat in flight. Her knotted, orange, untamable hair sticks out from her head like a detonated bag of party poppers. She is mannish, unhandsome, overweight – and we all love her like mad.

'Oh, Judy,' says Clare coming into the staffroom – Clare of the greasy dirty-blonde pigtails and potter's smock-frock. 'What've yer done?'

'I've only gone and stubbed my bleedin' toe.'

'Yer daft cow,' says Clare sympathetically.

Behind her, in the cloakroom, are Kay and Rez.

7

'Fuck fairies,' says Rez. 'Kids want sex, drugs, violence. Big fuck-off guns.'

'But . . . I like fairies,' says Kay timidly.

'Did someone say fairy?' says Phil, behind them. Then, to everyone, in his execrable French: 'Bonjour, may paytites.'

Phil is taking an evening class in French as he plans to live in a loft in Paris, where he can eke out a living as a painter by day and fuck lots of French boys at night.

'Bonjour, Philippe,' I reply.

'Ou est Marie-Claire?' says Steve sarcastically.

'Marie-Claire est gone to la boulangerie,' parries Phil, looking pleased with himself.

4

At 6.15 I wander upstairs to the top till. On my way up I bump into Iseult. 'How's my little Miffin?' she says, with – could it be? – *ill-suppressed sexual longing*.

'I'm, er . . . fine,' I bring out at last – flushed, weak-kneed. 'How . . . are you?'

'Late,' says Iseult, as she canters downstairs.

Of course, I'm in love with her. However, it wasn't love at first sight. When we first met I merely thought of her as being pretty. No, attractive. For Iseult (I'm fairly confident) is in her early thirties – and, after a certain age, say, twenty-five, women cease to be pretty. They can be beautiful, yes. Ravishing, sure. But not pretty. Iseult is tall, lissom, an avatar of grace – she seems to *glide* rather than walk. She has boyish bobbed blonde hair, green eyes, the lips of Jane Morris as rendered by Rossetti. Quite why, in the first few weeks, I was unaffected by her sultry late-night allure is a mystery to me. The only reason I can think of is that, back then, bookselling was still a bewildering business, for while I felt at home in the Fiction section, I was a total stranger to New Age, Craft and Self-Help books, and was simply too busy learning the ropes to pay heed to my libido. But as my booksellerly confidence began to grow, the old lusts and longings took hold, and, one night, chatting casually with Iseult, the God of Grand Folly shot an arrow through my heart and I was smitten.

5

At 6.30 the full-timers leave. Most nights they are bound for a publishing party of some sort; tonight is no exception: Outlandish Press are pleased to announce *In Your Face!*, more hair-raising tales of derring-do from Terry ('Nutter is my Middle Name') McNaughton, SAS veteran of the Gulf War, following on from the success of his first book, *Fuck With Me Not*. The Covent Garden branch of The Book Shop is notoriously unruly. We have a fine reputation for heckling, hard-drinking, fucking, puking, stealing – and, of course, substance abuse. Anyone who thinks bookselling is a fey profession would do well to attend a publishing 'do'. Only the other week a couple of full-timers, at a Transworld jamboree, were caught red-handed trying to spike Joanna Trollope's drink with LSD. Quite why the full-timers are all so ecstatically dissolute is unclear: perhaps it's because, like the part-timers, they once thought of themselves as artists – and, when drunk, still proclaim themselves as such – when in reality if there was ever a time when they practised their 'art' all they do now is sell books.

Cynthia, our dourly Christian manageress, a woman of giraffish ungainliness, clearly disapproves of her underlings' devil-may-care lifestyles – in her eyes we are insatiate sinners unamenable to redemption or grace. She seems, in rare moments of humanity, sincerely vexed that, for all our impiety and vice, we yet appear, at least when sober, to be ordinary, affable, semi-decent human beings.

Kay wanders over with a pile of books.

'What do *you* think of fairies?'

'I think they're a fabulous invention,' I say. 'An integral part of our fine folkloric tradition.'

She looks at me uncomprehendingly. 'I like them too,' she says.

Kay is twenty-eight. She is thin, fragile, childlike in the nicest, sprightliest sense – and for her age, unbelievably unspoilt. She is one of those people who believe that everyone is innately and immutably good. She herself has one of the kindest, gentlest, most trusting natures I've ever known outside of nursery school. In short, she is exactly the sort of person I'd always imagined wrote children's books. Her first book, *The Princess, the Pauper and the Romantic Fairy*

Godmother, is a delightful tale of true love transcending social differences in the Enchanted Land of Neverwhere.

'Why d'you ask?'

'Well, *Rez* said –'

'I wouldn't listen to Rez.'

'Why not?'

'He's . . .' I want to say: *full of shit*. Like most of the store detectives Rez claims to be a reconstructed gangsta. 'In the old days,' he told me once, 'I was known as the Baron of Brixton. *No* one fucked with me – and I mean *No One*: yardies, triads, even the Colombian cartels, I told 'em – "You fuckin' wid de wrong nigga". As for the po-*lice*: they's either on the payroll or they's too *scared* to touch me – the sorry sons of bitches.' So then why, I wondered, did Rez give it all up to become a store detective? 'I saw the light, man. I had "A moment of *clarity*" – just like the man say in *Pulp Fiction*.' I'd be more inclined to believe his story if it wasn't for the fact that I remember him from Montpelier, my primary school. Rez was in the year below, and sticks out in my mind as one of the few black children in the – by Brixton standards – consummately bourgeois suburb of Ealing. And then, when not bragging about his quondam career, Rez tends to speak English rather than Afro-American.

'He's a barbarian,' I tell her. 'He probably wouldn't know a pixie from an elf.'

'I like goblins,' says Kay. 'And sprites.'

'What are you *doing? Dawdling again?*' says Cynthia, suddenly upon us, like a hoydenish Akela reprimanding a couple of cubs. 'Chop-chop, Kay. Plenty of books to put out. And Miff –' desperately searching for a task – 'clean the till. It could do with a good tidy-up. There's a duster in the drawer.'

6

'D'yer wanna drink with us, then?' says Clare after work in what I can only – oxymoronically – describe as a species of civilised Scouse.

'I'd love one,' I reply.

We go to the Cross Keys on Endell Street. It is a balmy spring night, and we sit outside on the wooden picnic tables, surrounded by the high-spirited hubbub of other drinkers. Clare, in keeping with her earthy, artisanal lifestyle, drinks pints of bitter and chain-smokes spindly roll-ups of Drum.

Who, I wonder by way of conversation, are her favourite painters?

'I don't really 'ave any,' she says to my astonishment. 'I think people get bogged down tryin' to imitate what's already been done.'

'So . . . you're not influenced by painting?'

'Not really. Although there were a girl at school I sat next to. Katie Jenkins. If I 'ad to name an influence, I suppose it'd 'ave to be 'er. She did these mad swirly drawings – all pinks an' purples an' blues. They were dead trippy.'

'I take it this was at the Slade?'

'No. Primary school. She were only seven.' Then, responding to my open-mouthed amazement: 'For someone so intelligent, yer not 'alf daft at times yer know.'

'What . . .' I say, casting about for a question. 'What are you working on?'

'Well, for the past couple of weeks I've been attemptin' to do somethin' on chaos. I'm quite into the idea of randomness, yer see. All this week I've been pinchin' people's rubbish.' Then, defensively, as if sensing my surprise: 'I don't break into their 'ouse or anything, if that's what yer think.'

'Of course not.'

'I just nick the black bags people leave out for the dustmen. Then I empty them out onto the floor of me studio. And take photos.'

'Why?'

'Well, I think yer can learn a lot about people just by lookin' at their rubbish. I don't think people realise just 'ow intimate a thing rubbish is. The other day I found this letter. It were from this girl dumpin' 'er boyfriend. She said she couldn't stand the way 'e used to slobber all over 'er first thing in the mornin'. An' that every time 'e licked 'er face she got all spotty. An' that she didn't appreciate 'im takin' the piss out of 'er spots when 'e was the cause of 'em. An' that 'er spots were the cause of 'er low self-esteem. An' that was why she stayed with 'im. An' that on 'oliday with 'er mates she didn't 'ave any spots an' that she'd met someone else. Then at the bottom 'e'd written: I still love you, bitch.'

'Hmm. Interesting. But I still don't see what it's got to do with chaos.'

'Well, I think people's rubbish is a form of chaos – in a way. It's 'ard to describe. You'd 'ave to see it.' Then: 'I've got some photos back at me flat if you'd like to see 'em.'

'Really? I mean, if you're sure you don't mind.'

'Course not.'

7

Clare lives with three friends in a squat of indescribable squalor in King's Cross. Sitting on a mattress, amid the blasted debris of her bedroom, taking turns with a bottle of KwikSave Scotch, I can't help wondering why Clare in her quest for chaos didn't simply photograph her flat. Leafing through her photos, I'm quite taken with a pair of outsize orange underpants, with what looks to be a cigarette burn in the front.

'Good God. Whose are these?'

Clare looks up from the joint she is rolling, and says: 'They're great, aren't they? I like to think of 'em as belongin' to a wrestler.'

'I see what you mean. But don't you think taking photos in a way isolates them from the very chaos you're trying to capture? Imposes an order – as, indeed, art should?'

'Yer what?' she says, sparking up her spliff. Then, after holding the pungent bluish smoke in her lungs like a deep sea diver: 'Yer know what yer problem is, Miff?' exhaling noisily, her voice altered, sluggish, thick. 'Yer think too much. Yer always analysin' everythin'. Sometimes yer just got to let things be – without wonderin' why, or what for.'

Clare is much given to such pothead pronouncements – and whilst I ordinarily loathe pseudo-Buddhist hippie bull-shit, she imparts to it a sincerity and straightforwardness that I find, in spite of myself, tremendously appealing. She hands me the spliff, which, lest she think me square, I gingerly take a toke on. The first and last time I smoked dope I was sixteen years old. It was at a party in Kew and I was drunk for only the third or fourth time in my life, when the girl I'd been joylessly trying to pull all night offered me a 'jay'. We went out into the back garden, and, beneath the embowered pergola, sparked it up. Back then I didn't even smoke, and, once Camilla had pointed out how to inhale, I experienced an almighty headrush, and on the pretext of having a piss stumbled off into the shrubbery where I was audibly and unstoppably ill.

'*Miff,* yer *wastin'* it,' says Clare, mortified by my timid toke. ''Aven't yer ever puffed before?' Then, when I tell her my story: '*Ah*, yer so innocent.'

My pride pricked, I inhale greedily, and, as instructed, hold the smoke down for as long as I can. By and by I begin to feel disagreeably woozy and disoriented, as if reeling from some fiendish fairground ride. Extinguishing the roach in an empty can of Coke, Clare lights a couple of evil-smelling joss sticks, plugs in her lava-lamp, and switches off the light. Sitting down beside me on the mattress, she gives me a sweet albeit shitfaced smile, and says:

'I love yer.'

'I . . . love you too,' I say at last, at a loss to answer otherwise.

Pushing me back on to the mattress, she sits astride me, her arse chafing my crotch, and starts to kiss me. Her tongue is slippery and probing; her saliva sticky, hashish-sweet. At first I am too bewildered – half-drunk, semi-stoned – to be anything other than passive. She unbuttons my shirt, lifts off her smock, unclips her bra, and, squirting baby oil on my chest, gives me a massage. The feel of her humid hands kneading my flesh, the sight of her heavy lolling tits, the bracing infiltrating odour of the joss sticks, rouse me from my stupor, and I feel my cock stir and stiffen beneath her pulsating backside. I reach for her breasts, take their heft into my hands, then squash and manhandle them like so much playdough. A gleeful burble issues from the back of Clare's throat. Shuffling back on her knees, she unbuckles my belt and unzips my trousers, while I, slightly arching my back, free myself of my underwear. Standing up, she quickly steps out of her panties and trousers, and, kneeling down, her butt towards me, takes my rigid prick in her mouth. As she briskly, somewhat painfully fellates me, I grab hold of her arse with both hands, and, craning my neck, thrust my tongue into the juicy crucible of her cunt. Due to the extreme angle of my neck and her bobbing backside, my nose keeps coming up against her ticklish – all-too-literal – bumfluff; so, wriggling out from underneath her, I push her forward on all fours, and, kneeling, take her from behind. Her cunt is incredibly hot and wet, almost seems a separate entity, panting and gasping through the medium of Clare's mouth, and as we fuck I feel her juices trickle down my thighs until, after only a few minutes, belatedly remembering that we're having unprotected sex, I helplessly come inside her.

8

During the past twelve months I have had sex only twice: once with Clare, and, two weeks earlier, a ghastly one-night stand with my ex-girlfriend, Elizabeth. I met Liz at a Newnham bop. At the time she was going out with a rabid Trotskyite from King's, but he dumped her after she let slip that her dad was a Tory MP. And because Liz is one of those girls for whom a boyfriend is essential for a lively self-esteem, and hence has enjoyed a relay of men since the age of fourteen, the baton was handed to me. Looking back, the one thing we had in common was a mutual – in my case, unquenchable – lust for the other's body. And Liz was, let it be said, disembowellingly beautiful. Only, for all our pagan fuckfests, when fully clad I wanted nothing to do with her. She was pathologically incapable of living in the present – life would never again be as winsome and peachy as it was when she was . . . sixteen. Five. Seven. And she'd ramble on for hours about Crazy Larry's, ex-boyfriends, her goddamn teddy, seeing Matt Dillon in Henry J. Bean's – and never mind that I'd heard it all before. Her worst memory was of standing in her father's bedroom after he'd temporarily absconded with another woman, and saying: 'Where's Daddy?' The worst thing she had to confess – and, in her cups, she confessed it incessantly – was that her mother was an alcoholic. It's not so much that she lacked the decency to keep her mouth shut, but that she cynically ascribed all her failings and faults – and they were manifold – to these (as she put it) 'childhood traumas'. And then Liz was so quintessentially Cambridge, so rah-ish in every respect, a social butterfly whose female friends – Harrie, Henrie, Eddie and Fred – all had (once abbreviated) boys' names, that in retrospect I wonder that our relationship lasted as long as it did. She and her friends were part of a vampish drinking covey called the Newnham Nuns. It is hard to express here the swingeing contempt I felt for them: for while drinking 'copious amounts of Cinzano', getting '*heen*ously wrecked' and 'having randoms' – i.e. pulling people you've never met – are in themselves more or less innocuous, the ostentatious way they went about it, their supreme arrogance and hauteur, never failed to nettle – perhaps because, in a way, they seemed so sadly emblematic of the Cambridge student body. The most irritating thing about them, though, was their idiotic argot. 'Who Hugo?' one of them would say. 'He *absolutely* mings for England.' 'Oh, absolutely. Mings for Mars.' 'Yah, I agree. Hugo's biff.' 'Oh, you'll never guess what. Last night, I was absolutely *off my tits* at that awful cocktail thing at Clare. *And* . . .' 'What?' everyone would ask, collectively agog. 'I had a random with my random!' 'No!' 'Yes!' 'Eddie, you're *incorrigible*.' 'Hang on, you're not talking about that no-mark mathemo from Caius?' 'No.' 'The to-die-for comski at Downing?' 'What do you mean, "to-die-for"? He's an *ab*solute minger.' 'Really, Henrie, I simply can*not* locate my interest in your –' 'Oh, no, *I* know who you mean. You're thinking about that natski at Tit Hall.' 'Who *Rob?* He abso*lutely* mings for England.' Etc. etc.

Why, then, did I stay with her? I'm ashamed to say, I was

obsessed with her cunt. Indeed, I wasn't happy unless I had some part of my anatomy inside her – even something as seemingly unerotic as a big toe or an elbow or a thumb. And I would've gladly gone down on her for *days* if only she'd let me – if only she'd had the time. However, just when I thought I'd conquered this unsavoury vice, when my animosity towards her far outweighed her physical allure and I had at last resolved to end it, *she* dumped *me!* And, as if that wasn't bad enough, she subsequently went around telling everyone that she'd broken my heart and that, in a craven bid to keep her, I'd threatened to top myself. At the time (Michaelmas term, my final year) I was scandalised, and vowed to blank her thereafter. But when I bumped into her, a year on, one night after work, I thought it'd be churlish not to say hello. Liz was drunk and, back at my gran's place, launched into an obscenely sentimental nostalgia binge: how wonderful was her life at Cambridge, how nothing could ever be as wonderful again, how old she felt, how much she missed me, how seeing me again had brought it back – the view from her room at Newnham, the Bumps, punting on the Cam, bops, May Balls, formal hall ... And, so unstoppable were these cloying reminiscences, that, when I put my hand on her knee, she scarcely paused for breath; likewise, when I peeled off her panties and placed my head between her legs: indeed, her soliloquy only came to an end when we finally – belligerently – fucked.

9

'Talk about fucking *shameless*.'

Steve is holding the latest 'snow book', *Snow Gets in My Eyes*, ostensibly by A. Barbie Schultz, although doubtless penned by a roguish ghost writer jonesing on whisky and whizz. These days the publishing industry is every bit as conservative, derivative and altogether lacking in imagination as Hollywood. If a book is even halfway successful it will spawn a dozen imitations of itself: for instance, after the inexplicable éclat of *The Horse Whisperer* there came, in quick succession, *The Man Who Listens to Horses*, *The Horse Tamer*, *The Horse Trainer* and *The Horse Man*.

'First *Miss Smilla's Feeling for Snow*, then *Snow Falling on Cedars* – and now *this!*'

'You might want to think about putting snow in the title of your own novel,' I suggest.

'Yeah. Right. *The Death of Snow*.'

'You'll have to change your name though.'

'Why?'

'Not snowy enough. Insufficiently Scandinavian.'

'Alice Frost. Virginia Frigid.'

'And then there's the trend for pejorative feminine nouns. Joanna Trollope, Donna Tartt *et al*. Why not call yourself Carrie Slutt – with two 't's of course.'

'Vicki Vixen. Amanda Whore.'

As Steve rattles on, I am distracted by the sight of Iseult –

she is sitting at the Information Desk talking to Phil. *I love you
I love you I love you!* I have now to make a conscious effort to
repress these spontaneous outbursts of adoration, although I
fear that my love is an all-too-audible entity, that everyone
knows. Indeed, such is my paranoia that I become convinced
that Phil is telling Iseult of my gawky schoolboy's pash.
'Darling,' he seems to say. 'He's *deeply* smitten. Or, as the
French would say, armour foo.' Iseult laughs, obviously
pooh-poohing my passion.

'Miff?' says Steve enquiringly.

'Sorry. What?'

'*Subdolorous?*'

'Oh, yes. Subdolorous. It means crafty, doesn't it?' Then,
absently: 'Well done.'

10

Working on the premise that Iseult knows everything, I am
pointedly distant for the rest of the evening – although it
suddenly strikes me that my silence is just as eloquent of my
unrequited love as (in her presence) my awkwardness and
inarticulacy.

Towards the end of the evening, Iseult traps me on the top
till.

'*Miff,*' she purrs reproachfully. 'You're not ignoring me,
are you?'

Ignore you! I adore you! I'm madly in love with you! 'No,' I
reply. 'Why?'

21

'It's just, well, you've barely said hello to me all night.'

'I'm sorry. I've . . . been preoccupied.'

'With what, I wonder?'

'My new novel,' I lie.

'Oh yes,' she says expectantly.

'I'm sorry. I . . . I don't like to talk about my work. To paraphrase Hemingway, the more one talks about it the less compelled one is to do it.'

'I quite agree.' And indeed Iseult is famously enigmatic about her art. She refuses to tell anyone what she's working on and regards exhibiting as a form of painterly prostitution. 'Anyway, I wanted to ask you something.'

And I will make thee beds of Roses, / And a thousand fragrant poesies. 'What's that?'

'How would you feel about modelling for me?'

'Iseult' – *darling!* – 'I'd be honoured.'

'Well, that's settled then. Come round tomorrow,' handing me her card. 'Is one o'clock okay?'

'Fine.'

Just then the security gates emit their electronic shriek. Rez, who has been pretending to read the heartrending self-help book, *How to Cope with Blushing*, wheels around and, prodding a rigid forefinger into the offending gentleman's back, barks: 'Freeze, motherfucker!' Automatically the tottering old-timer raises his hands above his head. 'Okay. Assume the position. You know the drill.' Rez, spreading the old man's arms and legs, begins to frisk him. That done, he says 'Move-and-you-die', and proceeds to sift through the geezer's shopping bags. Cynthia, breathless from dashing up the stairs, cries: 'Rez, stop it. Stop it at once!' 'Stay back,' says Rez, waving his ID like a loaded gun. 'Store detective.' 'Store manager,' says Cynthia. 'Let this man go.' 'Aha!' – triumphantly producing a copy of *Fly Fishing* by J.R. Hartley – 'what have we here?' After examining the evidence, Cynthia says: 'I think you'll find, Rez, that that's a *library* book.' 'You shittin' me.' 'No, Rez, I am not.' Then, to the cringing pensioner: 'Sir, you have my *sincerest* apologies.' While Rez, obviously unconvinced of his innocence, says: 'Yo mama,' and contemptuously hands the book back.

11

After work I go back to Clare's. As soon as we step inside her room, we undress and have sex, as if observing some dispassionate protocol.

Lighting up a spliff, Clare lies back on the mattress, and, after a couple of ruminative tokes, says:

'Yer in love with Iseult, aren't yer?'

'I am not,' I say indignantly.

'Oh, Miff. Yer just like a little boy. 'Ere,' passing me the joint, ''ave somma this.'

'How did you guess?'

'Yer didn't make it 'alf obvious. If yer not gawpin' at 'er yer pretendin' to ignore 'er. And whenever yer near 'er, yer get all edgy an' distracted. Like tonight when yer were talkin' to Steve.'

'Christ. That bad, huh?'

'Well, it's 'ardly what I'd call subtle, no.'

Propped on one arm, looking at Clare, I absently exhale a speech bubble of smoke over her robust, matronly breasts.

'I'm sorry,' I say.

'About what?'

'I don't know. Iseult, I suppose.'

'What's there to be sorry for? I mean it's not as though we're goin' out or sommat.'

'So you're not miffed at me, then?'

'Course not.' I experience a mad rush of affection for her; taking the spliff, she says: 'Yer should've 'eard Judy today. She came up to me an' said: *Ooh*, I could murder a man. An' did I know any? Then she said she 'adn't 'ad sex for six months an' that the last time she'd done it were with a dwarf who worked at the UCL canteen.'

'Good God.'

'Then she said did I know if yer were single?'

'And what did you say?'

'I told 'er yer was.'

'Christ, Clare. Why did you say that? You know I get nightmares about her arse?'

'Yer what?'

'It's true. I do. For some reason – in my dream this is – I walk into the Ladies at work. There she is. There *it* is: Blancmangey, liquescent. Huge. I put my hand in, my arm – it *engulfs* me.'

'Agh, *Miff!*' protests Clare gleefully.

'All of a sudden I'm inside it. Like Odysseus in Polyphemus' cave. I'm trapped. I decide to look around. Then I meet this warty old woman, and when I ask her who she is, she

24

replies: I am the voice of Judy's arse. Then she asks me if I've got change for the phone. At the time this seems like a reasonable request, so I give her fifty pee. Then she pulls out a mobile, dials a number, and says: Don't worry, he's a little shit. Then, when she walks away, I notice she's got this big hole in the seat of her skirt, and that *her* arse, despite being an old woman, is just as comely as a sixteen-year-old's.'

'Yer dirty old perv.' Then, as I hook her legs over my shoulders and inch towards her breathy humid cunt: 'I'm 'alf tempted to do a montage of yer filthy little mind.'

'I'd like,' I mumble into her scratchy, mousy-brown pubes, 'to see you try.'

12

Iseult lives at the top of a large four-storey Victorian house off Hampstead High Street. Standing beneath the mock-Tuscan portico, I timidly depress the topmost buzzer – elliptically marked, unlike the others, with a lone initial: I. This, I reflect, is typical of Iseult, for her personal life, like her art, is shrouded in mystery, and discreet enquiries at work have yielded little in the way of fact – although, perhaps because she *is* so secretive, speculation abounds.

Iseult's voice, when she answers, despite the staticky intercom, is as huskily seductive as ever: '*Yes?*' she says, as if anticipating a lewd suggestion.

'It's me. Um . . . Miff.'

She buzzes me in.

In the hallway I have to remind myself, and my fidgety heartstrings, that I'm here simply to model, and that my runaway fantasies of this being but a necessary precursor to a perfervid affair are, after all, fantastical, improbable, the gaudy stuff of erotic daydreams. Halfway up the last flight of stairs I notice that the door to Iseult's studio is slightly ajar.

'Come in,' she says, after I knock.

I had half-expected her to greet me, poised before her easel, in a bespattered Klimtlike caftan. However, once inside her spacious studio, with its stripped floorboards and airy dormer windows let in to both sides of a steep mansard roof, I see she is wearing dark pinstriped trousers and a black silk shirt – and, while there is an easel in one corner, set before a large plan-chest, it is empty, and her materials are neatly stacked and capped, her brushes tidied away.

'Miffin,' she says affectionately. 'Come here, let me look at you.'

I move towards her gingerly, instantly regretting my choice of clothes – maroon jacket, black T-shirt, stonewashed jeans, leather brogues. Holding me at arm's length by the tips of her fingers, she regards me as if appraising an eccentric off-day Rodin.

'Er, Iseult,' I say, as she starts to fashion my body into various, one would hope, aesthetically satisfying forms.

'Yes.'

'Um. Hello,' is all I can think to say. Then, reverently gesturing at the mounted boards propped, with their backs toward us, against her plan-chest: 'I don't suppose, before we begin, I could take a look at some of your work. I mean of course if you don't want to I completely–'

26

'Fret not, Miff. I want you to see them. As a matter of fact, I . . .'

'What?'

'Now, close your eyes.' Keenly hoping that she'll be naked when I open them, I immediately obey. Then, moments later: 'Okay. You can look.'

Opening my eyes I am stunned to see that my prayerful hope has at least been partially fulfilled: for, directly in front of me, is a charcoal sketch of Iseult – rendered with unnerving fidelity in agitated Schielesque strokes – who, naked save for a pair of fish-net stockings, is enjoying a leisurely wank. It is entitled, at the bottom, in large childlike script: 'Mummy Indulging Herself with Three Fingers'. Iseult looks at me coquettishly. *What can this mean?* I start to say something, but she puts a finger to her lips. The next board, 'Breech Birth', depicts a patently unpregnant Iseult giving birth to a baby whose head, or rather mouth, is still nestled between her legs and, judging by the blissful expression on her face, provoking an unseemly amount of sexual pleasure. 'Baby in Space' has the infant floating, balloonlike, from its umbilical cord (which, from the aerial perspective, looks somewhat akin to a thin lumpy phallus), holding on for dear life to Iseult's erect nipples, who again is in the throes of erotic tumult.

Again I try to speak. Iseult presses her finger to my lips. Before I know it I am docilely sucking on her digit, stirred by some half-remembered instinct. Meanwhile, she has been unbuttoning her blouse, and, with all the casual unself-consciousness of a mother breast-feeding in public, produces her left tit and proffers it to me. *Oh my God.* This is hardly the scenario I'd envisaged. Iseult, though, is now coaxing my head towards her brown, semi-erect teat, and – what the hell – I take it in my mouth. I am relieved – and, too, obscurely disappointed – when my first tentative sucks fail to elicit an ejaculation of warm milk; for that is how I think of it, not as a stream, but in spurts, like hot creamy come, repeatedly fired into my mouth in one long unending orgasm. The idea excites me; I gnaw at her nipple like a gluttonous infant having sucked his mother dry, while blindly groping for her other breast with my left hand. Iseult seems delighted.

'*Oh*,' she cries, pulling back her blouse to reveal her right breast, its nipple already hard, expectant. '*Greedy* boy. My poor thirsty baby!'

I switch to her right tit, in my ardour roughly biting, gnawing, pincing. When I attempt to kiss her, she pulls away.

'You're sleepy, aren't you, baby?' she coos, nodding her head.

'Well –'

'*Ssh!*' she says, briskly slapping my backside.

'But –'

'*Naughty* boy!' Again the swift humourless slap. 'Now, let's get these clothes off, shall we?'

I allow myself to be led into the bedroom, and lie on the bed. If I remain mute while Iseult kneels at my feet and undoes my laces, removes my shoes and socks, as she carefully, tenderly undresses me, it is not for fear of her scolding slaps but lest she lose interest in the game altogether. As she leans over me in order to peel off my T-shirt, her hard tits jutting from her loose unbuttoned blouse, I clamp hold of her nipples like the airborne baby in her picture, provoking a play-reproachful *'Naughty boy'*. And by the time she herself disrobes, stepping out of her panties to reveal a demure isosceles triangle of sparse auburn pubes, I am so aroused, so irreducibly erect, that when she produces an outsized nappy from her bedside table, I slip it on. As a reward I am allowed to kiss her – shamelessly I slobber, shamelessly I lick, suck and caress, until my chin and cheeks are covered with our hot copious drool. Remembering 'Breech Birth', I slide down her body and press my mouth to the deckle-edged flower of her cunt; as Iseult spreads her legs I thrust my tongue inside her, as far as it will go; then, pulling out, trace the tip along her labia to the cowled apex of her clit, which I mercilessly tease, chafe and worry. After a while Iseult can stand it no longer, and, hooking her big toes into either side of my nappy, wrestles it down around my knees. Needing no more encouragement, I urgently free the nappy from my legs, and, scrambling forward – I flatter myself, deftly – shunt my cock into her cunt. 'Naughty Boy!' Iseult gasps, and, as I fuck her, with bitter-sweet abandon, she cries my new name in crescendo, until, buckling, arching, convulsed like a fish out of water, she screams 'NAUGHTY BOY!' and, drawing · blood from my back, judderingly comes.

13

'Matthew, is that you?' calls my grandmother (who, at seventy-eight, still has surprisingly keen hearing) as soon as I open the front door. 'Come here, would you. I'd like a word.'

For an insane instant, I am convinced that Gran knows everything. Knows that I've spent the afternoon in a nappy, making whoopee with my adoptive mum. Entering the drawing-room off the hall to the right, I find her in her regal rococo armchair, a copy of *Good Housekeeping* open in her lap. Her silver hair is thin and wispy, and up close one can discern her flaky mottled scalp. However, despite her frailty, her brittle bones, her hunched back and her foxed parchmenty skin, she is still a formidable woman, staring old age in the eye with indomitable dignity. Since her husband – a senior civil servant – died fifteen years ago, she has kept incredibly busy by playing bridge, browbeating lodgers, raising money for charity, and, finally and most all-consumingly, chairing her very own Association for the Appreciation of Charlotte Brontë. She and her group get together once a week and optimistically try to make sense of bombastic articles – 'Rights, Reason and Redemption: Charlotte Brontë's Neo-Platonism', 'Intimacy without Immolation: Fire in *Jane Eyre*' – before holding forth with heartfelt paeans of their own and, over coffee and cakes, having a good old gossip. When I was eighteen Gran came close to disowning me after I gave her my own glib assessment of *Jane Eyre* in which I complained that only after Mr Rochester is utterly emasculated does CB deign to reunite him with Jane – who, for all her supposedly 'passionate nature', I opined would be a spinster in the sack – unfavourably comparing the book to the flung Gothic intensity of her sister's precocious masterpiece *Wuthering Heights*, arguing (as I still do) that true love ends not in everlasting happiness but in deracinating tragedy.

'What is it, Gran?' I say, nervously sitting down on the edge of the divan.

'I want your opinion on Sapphism.'

'Sorry. I don't think I –'

'Sapphism. You know, it's when two women –'

'Gran, I know what it is.' Then: 'Why d'you ask?'

'Oh, Margery's gone off her rocker. She's going around telling all and sundry that . . . well, that she's one of them.'

'*No*,' I say, feigning outrage.

'The woman's eighty-three years old.'

'I don't believe it.'

'Of course . . . one's *heard* of Sapphism. But you don't really think . . .'

'Surely not. I always thought it was just something people made up to scare children – you know, like witches.'

'Well exactly. The very thought of it' – pantomiming nausea – 'makes me feel quite ill.'

'Oh, me *too*.'

'And to think, Marge was married for fifty years.'

Gran's friends all have delightfully old-fashioned names: Margery, Dorothy, Phyllis. Her husband's name was Cuthbert. They met one fine summer's evening at a dance; Gran caught him on the rebound: and, three months later, they were wed. So simple, so sweet. Indeed, theirs was seemingly a generation of uncomplicated courtship; straightforward romance. I rather doubt that I'll meet my wife under such innocent circumstances, that our journey to the altar will be as graceful or fleet. Although that doesn't stop me, on Underground platforms, scanning the carriages for my wife as the train comes to rest – and I'm still willing to believe that when I see her I'll somehow instinctively know: *she is the one*. That, due to some sidereal happenstance, we'll tumble into one another's arms.

'Oh yes, your mother called,' says Gran, with ill-concealed enmity.

'Oh no. What did she want?'

'She's in London. She says she wants to see you. You're to call her at . . . I forget now. I wrote it down. Some fancy hotel.'

'Did she say anything about my living with you?'

'Lord, no. It was all she could do to be civil. Spiteful hussy. Never did like her.'

'Yes. I know. You said.'

'Well,' peering at me querulously through the bottom of her bifocals, 'are you going to call her then?'

'I don't know.'

14

Up in my room – an ascetic affair with a bed, a desk, a modest wardrobe and a decidedly humble bookshelf (most of my books are still packed in boxes or piled on the floor) – I pour myself a Scotch and light a cigarette and with the old sad medley of emotions – resentment, anger, love, pity, dread – think about Theresa.

The last time I saw her was three years ago. She and her third husband – Bernie 'The Butterball King' McClintock – invited me to dine at the Savoy, having spent the summer aboard Bernie's palatial one-hundred-foot yacht flitting hither and thither between the fashionable resorts. Theresa, already unmistakably tipsy, was at first embarrassingly effusive. 'Miff, darling! *Mwuh!*' she cried, kissing me wetly on the lips. 'Darling, you look *won*derful. Really, *good enough to eat.* If it wasn't for Bernie, here – well, I don't know *what* I'd do.' Bernie (whom I'd never met, despite the fact that he and my mother had by then been married for more than a year) turned out to be an amiable, not unhandsome, man in his mid-fifties. 'How you doin', fella?' he said, simultaneously clapping me on the back and shaking my hand. 'Fine, thanks, Bernard,' I tartly replied. 'How are you?' 'Great. Just great.' Then: 'Tessy's told me a lot about you.' 'Oh really. Like what?' 'She told me you like books. Here. I got you this,' handing me a copy of *How to Win Friends and Influence People* by Dale Carnegie. 'It may not be D.H. Lawrence but it sure taught me a thing or two.' But if Theresa began by making a fuss of me – holding my hand, ordering champagne, besieging me with compliments and questions – she grew increasingly testy during the meal (she scarcely touched her Waldorf salad and refused to order anything else), sulkily chain-smoking while Bernie held forth on the highpoints of their cruise – St Tropez, Cannes, Monte Carlo – speaking only to contradict him ('It's pronounced *Ricard*, you oaf, not Richard') or to criticise me ('Darling, where on *earth* did you get that suit? Marks and Spencer's?'). After the meal, though, while Bernie messily incinerated a Monte Cristo, she perked up, and, now mawkishly drunk, told me how much she loved me and how ardently she and Bernie both hoped that I'd come to visit them in Palm Beach, she'd been so busy

33

since the wedding but now that they were settled there was no excuse for not keeping in touch. But I'd heard it all before; I knew she'd never change. And while there was a time – call it my childhood – in which I'd passionately clung to her promises (as soon as she'd worked things out with her latest husband or beau I could come and live with them in their spangled foreign paradise), there came a point when the prospect of yet another bitter letdown was so unbearable that I ceased believing altogether, banished from my heart those dreams she'd so cruelly nurtured, then betrayed. And whereas in the past, on the infrequent occasions that we met – it wasn't uncommon for years to elapse between visits, months to pass without so much as a postcard or a call – I'd done my best to hurt her, in the end it was simply easier to be polite, less upsetting to affect forgiveness. However, at the time I too was drunk – I'd spent the afternoon in a nearby bar steeling myself for the encounter – and, lashing out, said: 'What about Sarah? Is *she* invited, too? I'm sure she'd be *thrilled.*' 'Of . . . Why of course,' she replied, palpably panicked, alarmed. Then, to my sickened disbelief, Bernie said: 'Who's Sarah?'

15

Sarah is my younger sister. At the age of eighteen she can neither read nor write. She cannot walk, can only barely talk; has defective hearing and vision. Her limbs are so gnarled and stiff she cannot feed herself – she is, indeed, entirely dependent on other people's benevolence for her simplest, most fundamental needs. As if these disabilities were not bad enough, she is also mentally retarded; mercifully, though, this means that she is less aware of the acute frustrations and limitations experienced by spastics of ordinary intelligence.

As a child I was deeply ashamed of my sister. The few friends I had were never invited to play at my house (I'd pretend that my mother was sick, or that my father forbade it – indeed, devised any number of different excuses over the years) lest they catch sight of Sarah – with her thick glasses and her bulky hearing aids, slumped in her wheelchair in an attitude of profound and tortured helplessness – lest they hear her tantrums and screams. And how I hated Joey Deacon, the pet spastic of *Blue Peter*, who, in foisting his disability on the stony hearts and minds of children, created there not compassion, nor comprehension, but ridicule and contempt – inadvertently made of cerebral palsy a laughing stock. Suddenly, everyone had heard of spasticity, *Blue Peter* acquired a cult following, and for the next three years all I seemed to hear were jubilant cries of 'spas' or 'spasmo', or deft impersonations of Joey himself which my classmates found unflaggingly hilarious and at which I too (so as not to attract suspicion) forced myself to laugh. If anything, though, the *Blue Peter* campaign highlighted my hypocrisy, made me feel ashamed of feeling ashamed, for I frequently felt towards my sister an aching tenderness and love, only these fine emotions were all-too-quickly tempered by anger and resentment, as such were the demands her disability made upon my father (Theresa walked out on us not long after Sarah was diagnosed as having cerebral palsy) that I inevitably felt cheated of my share of affection and love – and, moreover, at a time (in the aftermath of my mother's abandonment) when I needed them the most.

As I grew older, my attitude changed. I became defiantly proud of her meagrest achievements – the painstaking, ultimately negligible, progress Sarah made at her special day-care school. But where once I'd felt shame, there now dwelt guilt: *Why Sarah? Why not me?* For Theresa had refused to quit smoking or drinking when she was expecting both Sarah (an unwanted pregnancy on which my father, for once, had stubbornly stood his ground) and me; but whereas I was born more or less on schedule, Sarah arrived three weeks premature – a tiny outcast whose chances of survival were, at best, slim. Thus, in my teenage years, I felt beholden to shine twice as brightly, to work twice as hard, to exploit to the uttermost the potential that Fate had so arbitrarily imbued in me and denied Sarah. I would, in short, be brilliant for both of us. And, at least academically speaking, brilliant I was. Straight A's at St Paul's. A scholarship to St John's. A First from Cambridge. However, my assiduity cost me dear. At school, while not exactly friendless, I mostly kept to myself: back then I would've maintained that I was too damn busy and ambitious to waste my time on parties, girls and getting wrecked; although I now see that this is partially true, my stoicism had more to do with feeling unentitled to those sensual pleasures that my sister would never know. And at Cambridge I was similarly monkish, indeed, approached my studies with a missionary zeal; and while everyone else was seemingly whooping it up at the Anchor, the Eagle, Global and Sin, or (on Tuesday nights) slumming it at Cindy's, I was soberly reading in my room. And for those who still subscribe to the fallacy that getting a First is merely a matter of being what's romantically known as 'naturally brilliant', what's actually involved is, prosaically enough, working one's arse off. But if I failed to forge any lasting male friendships it wasn't simply due to my industry, nor to my highminded frowning on fun, it was because I felt little or no affinity with the males that I met – I wasn't interested in sports, I remained aloof from college rivalries, I didn't care for drinking cliques, pub crawls, rites-of-passage puking up – and was consequently seen as eccentric and effeminate, at worst reviled as an out-and-out fag. As for women, aside from Liz, I had a couple of indifferent one-night stands. It is perhaps worth mentioning one in some detail, for it has by now ignominiously entered Cambridge folklore.

One Friday night, feeling frisky, I picked up a Kiwi undergraduate named Ally in the John's bar. Now, as a rule, I never carry condoms, the theory being that those who tote them around on the off-chance that they might get laid never in actuality do – and what's more pathetic or reproachful than an out-of-date johnny belly-up in the bottom of one's wallet? Only when you've all but agreed to whump each other senseless is it permissible to sidle up to the Durex dispenser in the bogs. However, on this occasion, it slipped my mind, and of course Ally didn't have any (if she had, true to my theory, she wouldn't have pulled). While brushing my teeth I rehearsed my earnest I-promise-I-won't-come-inside-you speech; returning to my room, though, I discovered Ally passed out naked on the bed. After trying unsuccessfully to rouse her, I got undressed, turned off the light and got in. By and by, unable to sleep, my cock boring a hole in the bedsheets, I caved in to the lesser of two temptations and began to masturbate. Halfway through, like a clap of thunder in the dark, Ally (obviously woken by my stirring self-abuse) suddenly boomed: 'Have yi slimed yit, mate? If not, whack it up mi shitter.' The next morning, itching to tell someone what she'd said, I recounted the story to Frank, my next-door neighbour. That afternoon, standing in line at the buttery, I overheard a total stranger quote Ally word for word. A little later, in the UL, one of the librarians was at it. As were the porters, when I stopped by my pigeonhole, and the barstaff of the Eagle later that night. The next day, in the laundry room, someone told *me*. And within a week what'd started out as an at best amusing anecdote had taken on the apocryphal aura of myth.

16

There is a knock at my door. I have forgotten all about my lesson with Anthony. 'Come in,' I say. Anthony is wearing a short-sleeved shirt, white chinos, and, clearly visible above his suede Hush Puppies, white towelling socks. 'Anthony! You crazy hepcat, you.'

'Um. Sorry?' Then, gazing with frank dismay at the bottle of Johnnie Walker on my desk, the overloaded ashtray: 'I have got the right day?'

'Yes, you have. Excuse me. I'm . . . all over the place.'

'So I see,' he says boldly.

'And what's that supposed to mean?'

'Nothing.' Then: 'D'you often drink by yourself?'

'Depends what you mean by often,' I say evasively.

'Every day?'

'Um. Most days, yes.'

'But it's bad for you. Why would you drink when you know it's bad for you?'

'It's not . . . bad for you,' I say like an ageing dopefiend lethargically defending his chosen drug.

'It is. It is in large quantities. Sclerosis of the liver kills thousands every year – *tens* of thousands.'

'I'm still alive, aren't I?' now annoyed.

'D'you drink in the mornings?'

'Okay, I admit it. I'm a hopeless alcoholic. I've got bottles stashed all over the house. When I'm at work I take hits from a hipflask in the toilets. I eat Clorets to disguise the smell of meths on my breath.'

Somewhat startled: 'I was only asking.'

'Now,' I say, secreting the bottle of Scotch in a desk drawer, 'let's see that essay on Joyce.'

17

'Philippe! Ma cherie! Comment ça va?' I say, entering the staffroom.

'Oh *Miff*. Er . . . "bean mercy".' Then: 'Oh yes. Um. Et voo? Or, dare I presume, too?'

'Oh, pas mal, pas mal.'

'You're awfully good at French, Miff. Have you lived *en*

français?'

'God no. Although I've been to Paris a couple of times.'

'O Parry, Parry! Mon future *domicile.* I can see it now. Promenading en le *Left Bank.* Drinking absinthe in bohemian bars. I'm even thinking about changing my name. What d'you think to Philippe Aujourd'hui?'

'Oh, very *French,*' I say, nodding sagely. Then: 'I don't suppose you've seen Iseult, have you?'

'No. I don't think she's in yet.' Then, lowering his voice confidentially even though we're the only people present: 'I'll tell you *what.* You can keep a secret, can't you, Miff?'

'Absolutely. Anything.'

Having checked the cloakroom for potential eavesdroppers, Phil says: 'I think I'm falling in love with her. Iseult, that is.'

'But Phil,' I protest, 'you're a screaming homosexual.'

'I *know*, it's terrible. But what can I do? I'm obviously a closet straight.'

'I can see I'm going to have to out you.'

'Oh no you *can't.* You *ab*solutely mustn't. I mean, what would my mother say?'

'Well of course it'd come as a shock. But, you know, after a *while* . . . I'm sure she'd get used to it.'

'But . . . it's so un*natural.* So *deviant.*'

'Oh Philippe, how can you say that? It's been going on since time immemorial. Even the *Greeks* did it. Odysseus, Hector, Achilles – they *loved* it.'

'Really?' says Phil hopefully.

'Really. There's nothing to be ashamed of. I mean –'

Just then I spy Victoria hanging up her coat. 'Miff,' she

says, rushing into the staffroom. 'I've made a breakthrough! A real breakthrough!'

'Hello to you too,' says Phil, slightly piqued.

Ignoring him, she sits next to me and, with considerable effort, hoists her satchel on to her lap. Up close her sallow skin is coarse and papery; her once-chestnut hair wiry, lustreless, dry. 'I was thinking about what you said. You know, about my work being antiquated?'

'Well, that's not *exactly* what I –'

'Here. Read this.'

As I read through Victoria's poem Steve, Judy, Iseult and Clare clatter in and help themselves to coffee.

'Shocking, isn't it?' she says as soon as I look up, although the only shocking thing about 'Hamburger Fatty' is that Victoria – outwardly so prim and fastidious – could've written so forthrightly about the queasy co-existence of desire and disgust.

'Well,' I say, attempting to be tactful, 'it's certainly, um . . . more *emancipated* than your previous work.'

A fearful silence descends as Cynthia enters the room. She is wearing a mannish charcoal-grey business suit, with inappropriately brawny, Sue Ellen-style shoulder pads.

'Now, who's missing?' As if mentally ticking off a register, she scans the room. I attempt to catch Iseult's eye in order to exchange a clandestine lovers' look. Iseult, though, is gazing absently at the swirling scum on her instant coffee. 'Kay? Where's Kay? Well, has *any*one seen her?' She stares at us accusingly, as if implying her absence is somehow our fault. 'Goodness! Didn't anyone *remind* her of the meeting tonight?' Again, our silence seems guilty, complicit. 'Typical! Oh well.

41

I'll have to start without her. Now, as you all know, Terry McNaughton –'

'Nutter!' heckles Steve, grunting like a squaddie.

'Really, Steven. Do be quiet. I simply won't stand for any more of your *inane* interruptions.' The *inane* was enunciated with palpable relish, another instance – if only in her own mind – of her dazzling diction. 'Now, as I was saying, Terry McNaughton is giving a reading tonight. Patricia and myself will be taking care of Mr McNaughton and the Outlandish reps. So I expect you part-timers to take care of the running of the shop. Above all, don't interfere. And, for goodness sakes, don't, I repeat *don't*, drink the wine. We all know what happened last time.' (Steve, having bolted a bottle of Asti Spumanti in the bogs, decided to give an impromptu reading in the children's section, drunkenly declaiming racy passages from *Crash* to the assembled audience of awestruck four- and five-year-olds.) 'Now. Moving on. There've been a number of till *discrepancies* of late –'

'So then *I* said,' says Rez, presumably to Kay, in the cloakroom, 'I goes: You best kill me, motherfucker. You best kill me now. Coz if you let me *live*, I'm gonna track you down, and by the time me and the brothers done finished with you you's gonna wish *yo* sorry ass never got *borned*.'

18

Upstairs in the children's section, Iseult hands me a note. Expecting some thrilling declaration of love, it is with immense disappointment that I read: 'Tell Naughty Boy to meet me tomorrow at 2 pm. Perhaps you could take him. If not put him in a taxi – I'll pay. His mummy misses him. – I.' I had hoped that, having proved my willingness to submit to her unorthodox fetish, Iseult and I could at least act like normal lovers in the outside world. In the staffroom, though, she barely acknowledged me, and, without returning my hello, disappeared before I'd even read her note. And this after I'd spent most of last night feverishly looking forward to snatched kisses in the stockroom, sly caresses on the shop floor, reckless lovemaking in the ladies' lavatory.

Finally, half an hour later, unable to wait until my break, I impetuously desert my station – a sackable offence – and go downstairs in search of Iseult. I find her in the travel section. Terry McNaughton, surrounded by a semi-circle of fawning fans, is coming to the peroration of his reading. Behind the lectern there is an enormous poster of Nutter in combat fatigues wielding an immense sub-machine-gun.

'"Those sand wogs won't fuck with us again," I said to Frank. "No," he replied. "I guess they won't."'

After an enthusiastic round of applause, one of the Outlandish reps – a pretty blonde in her early thirties – announces that Terry has graciously agreed to field questions from the floor, after which he'll be only too happy to sign copies of either *Fuck With Me Not* (now available in paperback) or of course *In Your Face!* (hardback, £15.99).

'Look, Iseult,' I whisper, once the Q&A session starts. 'You don't think you're taking this whole Naughty Boy business a bit too far?'

'Who's Naughty Boy?' she replies, her voice icy, indifferent.

You know damn well who he is, I'm about to say when Cynthia glowers at me evilly.

Just then Steve taps Iseult on the back, signalling that it is time for her break. As I watch her walk away, fairly swooning with loss, I grab hold of Steve's arm to steady myself.

'Asymptotically,' he whispers.

Heartened, I whisper back: 'Infundibular.'

'Yes,' says Nutter, pointing to his next interlocutor. 'Gentleman at the back.'

'There's been rumours in the press that you're writing a novel. Is this true?'

Terry – a bulky, thickset man in his mid-forties, with a two-inch crewcut and an incongruously queeny moustache – exchanges a knowing glance with the blonde from Outlandish. 'Yes. It is,' he says, stifling a chuckle.

'Christ,' says Steve, *sotto voce*. 'Like it's not bad enough he's writing fucking book reviews for the goddamn *Guardian*.'

'As you may have heard, *In Your Face!* was subject to government censorship. As a result of which I was forced to cut some of my best material. So Cathy Atkins – my editor – suggested I try a fictional account in order to incorporate the lost material.'

'Yeah. Right,' says Steve. Then, putting his hand up: 'What's your take on structuralism?'

A delicious flicker of incomprehension crosses Nutter's face. 'Basically,' he says after a long thoughtful silence, 'I'm distrustful of literary theory. I'll allow that the idea . . . of the authorless text . . . is an intriguing one. But speaking as an author . . . it's also something of an insult.'

'No *way*,' says Steve incredulously.

Suddenly Cynthia is on top of us. 'What are you *doing?*' she hisses.

'Nothing.'

'Kay,' I find myself saying, 'needs some change. For the top till.'

'*Now?*'

'She said it was urgent.'

'Oh, *okay*. What does she need?'

'Um. Pounds and pennies.'

'I'll have to fetch them from the safe.' Then, glaring at Steve: 'I'll *deal* with you later.'

Nutter, in response to another question, says: 'Nothing's been decided as yet, but I was thinking about calling it *Operation Headfuck*, although I know Cathy's got her heart set on *Desert Snow*.'

With Cynthia out of earshot, I raise my hand. 'Two-part question, this. What was William Faulkner's last published novel? And, for a bonus point, in what year did it appear?'

'Um. Let's think . . . That would have been . . . *The Reivers*. And it appeared in . . . 1962.'

'Good God. He's right,' I say to Steve.

'Don't worry. We'll get this fuck.'

Ignoring Steve's outstretched arm, Nutter calls on Rez.

'What's in the briefcase in *Pulp Fiction?*'

'Ah, that would be . . . Marsellas Wallace's soul,' Nutter replies, his forehead furrowed in concentration. 'In the first scene with Bruce Willis he's wearing a bandaid on the back of his head. Later on though . . . once John Travolta and

Samuel L. Jackson have retrieved the briefcase from the kids
. . . the bandaid is conspicuously absent. I believe there's a
section . . . in the King James bible –'

As Nutter . . . falteringly . . . proceeds to explain the
technicalities of selling one's soul to the devil, I notice that
he's wearing an earpiece – such as might be found on a TV
presenter or an agent of the FBI. Stealthily, I make my way
towards Cynthia's office and, having entered the security
code, edge my head around the door. Sitting at Cynthia's
desk (on which there are arrayed two encyclopaedias and
numerous works of reference) I discover a man wearing
headphones, hunched over a mike. 'Thus,' he whispers, his
back towards me, 'the emphasis on Samuel L. Jackson's
spiritual redemption.'

Undetected, I withdraw my head and close the door, just
in time to hear Terry say: '. . . Thus the emphasis on Samuel
L. Jackson's spiritual redemption.'

'What,' I say in Latin, without waiting to be asked,
determined to scupper the operation, 'is the title of Vladimir
Nabokov's last unpublished novel, and how many pages had
he written at the time of his death?'

Terry's face, as he waits in vain for an answer ('Um. Let's
see . . .' he says), clouds with a satisfying anxiety and panic. I
shoot Steve a sly, triumphal wink; behind his hand, he silently
mouths, *He's fucked.*

Meanwhile, Judy, seemingly on her own initiative, has
gained the lectern, pre-empting the Outlandish rep who –
halfway out of her seat – was just about to come to Terry's
rescue.

'On behalf of The Book Shop,' says Judy in a jittery voice,

all but baffled by a burst of high-frequency feedback, 'I'd like to thank Terry and his colleagues at Unlawful Press. So, ladies and gentlemen, without further, um, to do, let's give it up for Nutter McMoron!' After a smattering of uncertain applause, she continues: 'Thank you. And now I'd like to ask Nutter' – who, visibly bewildered, is being led to a chair – 'a question of my own. What're you doing on Friday night? And, if nothing, how's about a curry?'

'I'd, um . . . be delighted,' he says at last, still shaken by the turn of events.

Flushing violently, Judy rejoins: 'The pleasure, Nutter, is mine.' Then, after a hasty, off-mike tête-à-tête with Victoria: 'And now, for your sumptuous enjoyment, The Book Shop is proud to present its resident poetess, Victoria Byron!'

'I thought her name was Jenkins,' says Steve.

'It is. Byron's her *nom de plume.*'

As Victoria makes her way to the lectern – to the scattered applause of The Book Shop staff – Patricia rushes from the room, doubtless in search of Cynthia.

'Thank you, thank you,' says Victoria, as if to a full house of zealous fans. 'The poem I'd like to read for you today is entitled "Hamburger Fatty".' *Oh no*, I think. *Oh no!* As she shakily unfolds her poem, she appears freakish, storklike, perilously pale. She coughs. '"Hamburger Fatty".'

> I see you on the number nine bus
> Glutting yourself with burgers and fries
> The mustard on your mouth appears like pus
> The ketchup, blood – another animal dies

Yet I stare at the breadcrumbs littering your crotch
Your manhood limned against your leg
My heart misgives me like a faulty watch
Dear God, I pray, don't make me beg

And though I should hate your rank burger breath
Your murderous mortal jaws
I yet dream of being your bounden chef
Meaty coitus on the kitchen floor

As Victoria launches into the fourth stanza ('And if it please you, we'll use lard for a lubricant/ Sheep's intestine as a prophylactive'), Cynthia storms into the room and cries, 'Victoria! What are you *doing*? For the love of God, child, stop!' 'And afterwards we'll sacrifice a ruminant' she continues, raising her voice, unfazed by Cynthia's fury: 'And make to the gods an offering substantive!'

19

Iseult is fairly overjoyed to see me. As soon as I set foot inside her studio, she strips off all my clothes and fits me with a nappy. Of course I try to protest, attempt to speak – but such unbabylike behaviour is met with the smarting reprobation of her riding crop. Not only am I not allowed to talk, it also transpires that I'm forbidden to smoke, walk, or to perform even the simplest tasks by myself. Thus she feeds me milk from a bottle, combs my hair, even takes me to the toilet – liberally wiping my willy afterwards. Indeed, it is only during sex that I'm granted any kind of autonomy; and, having been so thoroughly unmanned, I'm at pains to assert myself in the sack. But if at first I merely go through the motions in order to get laid – by and by, as my inhibitions unbend, I come to relish being babied, being so frankly and slavishly adored, even the crack of her riding crop now carries an erotic charge.

Halfway through the afternoon, such is my need for a cigarette, that, much to Iseult's delight, I deliberately guzzle all her milk, and, like many another insatiate terror, bawl my eyes out. 'Hush now, Naughty Boy,' she coos. 'Mummy's going to the shops.' Then, crouching down to tousle my hair: 'Mummy go milk-milk.' As soon as she leaves I scramble to my feet, and, in the bedroom, pounce on Iseult's packet of Silk Cut. Gazing at the ravaged bedsheets, I lightly finger an immense damp patch – a gloopy island of spent bodily fluids. My fingers, when brought to my nose, smell yeasty, agreeably sour; yet prove, when licked, to be relatively tasteless. Turning my attention to the room at large I am struck by a lingering unlived-in quality: the white walls are naked, the wardrobe, behind its painted wooden laths, yields nothing save for a couple of coathangers, even the bedside table is empty, its drawers bare. Suddenly curious, I quit the bedroom and try the drawers of her plan-chest: the topmost one is empty, the others locked. Even the kitchen nook, betrays scant signs of life: a couple of glasses, a mug, a half-drunk bottle of Chablis (which, after a couple of swigs, begins to curdle the milk in my stomach), a jar of Nescafé, a couple of teaspoons, a kettle. No food. However, in one of the drawers, alongside some small change and a carton of Silk Cut, I find three loose photos. The first is of a baby lying in its cot, serenely sucking on a dummy: fair hair, blue eyes, indeterminate sex – aged (approximately) six to eight weeks. The next photo shows Iseult (somewhere in her teens, with long, straight, mousy-brown hair) holding the same infant in her arms – and whilst I strain to discern some sort of family resemblance, he/she, to my untutored eye, merely looks like a baby: big-headed, wispy-haired, puffy, pink. In the third photo the baby is revealed as a boy: held aloft by Iseult – her face, in profile, transfigured with joy – his tiny wizened winkie is clearly visible. But because the infant's features were obscured in both 'Breech Birth' and 'Baby in Space', it is impossible to tell whether the one was modelled on the other. Indeed, the photos, far from illumining Iseult's fetish, render it yet more murky and opaque: Whose baby is it? I wonder. (Iseult, so far as I can tell, doesn't have stretch marks.) And, more troublingly: *Where* is it? Is it missing? Alive? Dead?

Upon hearing the rusty shriek of the garden gate, I rush to the window. I see Iseult walking up the drive clutching a skimpy carrier-bag. Stubbing out my cigarette, I open a window, replace the photos and clamber back into my nappy. When Iseult arrives I am curled up on the bed, thumb in mouth, pretending to sleep. She sits down beside me on the bed and rubs my tummy. 'Naughty Boy. Look,' tickling my nose with the teat of the milk bottle, 'look what Mummy's brought.' Ignoring the milk, I thrust my hand up her skirt, and tug her panties down around her knees. 'Naughty Boy!' Iseult scolds. But Naughty Boy has already hoiked up her skirt and ensconced his head between her legs, filling his lungs with the sweet dry-cleaning smell of her pursed, perennially parted, cunt.

20

After we have sex it is time for my lesson. Iseult sits me on the floor of her studio, and, unlocking one of her plan-chest drawers, removes several boards. 'Now,' she says, 'Mummy's going to teach you the alphabet. We want to learn the alphabet, don't we? *Yes.*' Smiling, ruffling my hair. 'Okay. A' – placing the corresponding picture on the easel – 'is for Apple.' And, lo, Iseult has drawn in hazy pastels two dozen faux-naif apples in the shape of an 'A'. In my limited capacity to compliment, I can only clap my hands. 'And B' – swapping the pictures – 'is for Bear.' Looking up I see a wonderfully fluffy golden teddy bear, rendered in gouache and ink, with artful black dabs for eyes and nose and paws, wearing a fetching red T-shirt emblazoned with a 'B'. Even at a glance it is clear that Iseult has invested a considerable amount of time and effort into each picture, which isn't to say that they appear effortful – on the contrary her style is bold, unworried, crisp – merely that they seem so palpably cared-for, loved. 'And C . . . is for Cat.' As I admire Iseult's splendid Cornish Rex, again in gouache and ink, curled up in the shape of a 'C', I am reminded of my own – foredoomed – attempts to educate my sister. Quite why I thought I'd succeed where experts in the field had failed – the whole army of speech- and occupational- and physiotherapists who catered to Sarah's needs – I don't know. But every so often, in an access of unbeckoned optimism, I'd rush into her room and take up her blackboard and write the letter 'A', besides which I'd draw an apple. 'A,' I'd say to Sarah, over and over. 'Ma-ooh,' she'd reply – her approximation of Matthew – her head canted round to the right so that it snagged on her shoulder. When the alphabet failed, I'd try numbers, colours, names. Until, finally, oftentimes weeping with frustration – for her helplessness, and my helplessness to help her, filled me with despair – I'd be forced to admit defeat. And there were days when the sight of Sarah (say, after a convulsive seizure in which she'd shat herself) was so intolerable that I actually thought about killing her, ending her (to me) sad embattled life. 'D,' says Iseult, 'is for dog.' But perhaps Sarah's really is a blissful ignorance – for my knowledge of the world, such as it is, has been largely disillusioning.

Shit. There've been days when I thought about killing myself . . .

21

When I arrive home there is a message from my grandma: 'Matthew, Reginald [her bridge partner] and I have gone to trounce those rank amateurs the Norfolks. Your mother called. She is becoming most bothersome. Please call her at the Regent Hotel. Love Gran.' Next to her note, on the occasional table in the hall, is a parcel addressed to me. Upstairs in my room, having poured myself a Scotch, I tear open the Jiffy Bag and pull out a book: *The Unspeakable Taboo*, by Constance Fitzrovia. Delicately – for it is falling apart – I turn to the title page: first published by Smith, Elder & Co. in 1872, it was reissued by Penguin (the tatty paperback edition I hold in my hand) in 1954. Initially mystified, I now remember that, not long after I started working at The Book Shop, I'd asked Iseult to name her favourite novel. The answer was so impassioned and emphatic I dared not confess to never having heard of Ms Fitzrovia. 'Hmm. Interesting,' I think I said, before running off to look her up on Whitaker's; however, as I'd feared, my search proved fruitless, and, rather than asking Iseult to lend me her copy – and thereby admitting that I'd never read it – I filled out a second-hand book search form, crossed my fingers and waited. But that was more than a month ago, and I'd since given up expecting to hear anything.

22

Book One describes the heartrending childhood of our heroine, Necessity Channing. Her father, Wilkie, owns a cotton mill in —field, a prosperous industrial town in the equally enigmatic county of —shire. Her mother is an Unrivalled Beauty, who, for all her pagan charms, is yet a Christian of constancy and charity – and, possessed of a sturdy intellect withal, she is also a notable belletrist. Irked by her reproachful piety and all-round perfection, this (relentlessly apostrophised) reader was mightily relieved when she died in the throes of childbirth. Alas Sebastien, Necessity's brother, survives – an infuriating, improbably precocious tyke of 'angelic aspect', who, at the age of eight, says things such as: 'Dearest Necessity, I fear you err, —field cathedral has curvilinear tracery; the geometric style to which you refer resembles two contiguous lancet windows surmounted by a quatrefoil.' As befits his consumptive sensitivity, Sebastien, much given to somnambulism, sleepwalks a full half league in the pouring rain, wakes up, catches cold and dies of pneumonia. Necessity is of course devastated. 'For two whole days she wept without respite; her wracking sobs knew no issue: and so pitiful and plaintive were her divers laments that Bessie [her nurse] feared that her poor heart must rend in twain.' Finally, after a precarious period of mourning in which it looks as if she will surely follow her mother and brother to the grave, Necessity pulls through, spurred on by the thought that if she too dies her father'll be utterly bereft.

Book Two finds Necessity a full grown woman – radiant, intelligent, and of course singularly beautiful. Ere too long she is being wooed by the local clergyman – an unprepossessing man who, in the face of sundry suitors, yet wears her down with his canine tenacity and ominous intimations of what Necessity will suffer in the hands of someone less spiritually endowed. However Necessity, having promised her hand to the Dowdy Cleric, is fairly swept off her feet by a Handsome Stranger who swans into town. 'And what palpitations of the heart did Necessity know in his presence, – what ecstasy! what sweet happiness! what joy! – to perambulate her father's estate on his arm, to hear in his voice all the affection and ardour she requited in kind

with every particle of her being.' She breaks off her engage-
ment to the Dowdy Cleric – who, after a show of
magnanimity, retires to the rectory and there invokes all
the direful maledictions known to man – and, scant weeks
later, is married to the Handsome Stranger, Mr Montagu
Gloucester.

Once married, Mr Gloucester proves a cad – gone is the
gallantry and charm, the noble sentiments, that had so
impressed Necessity in the halcyon days of their courtship.
Not wanting to upset her father, though – who is dying of
TB – she endeavours to appear happy and content, suffering
Mr Gloucester's rampant dissipation and multiple foibles of
the flesh with exemplary, well-nigh saintly fortitude. After
the birth of their son, Sebastien, such is Wilkie's grandpater-
nal joy, that he makes a miraculous recovery – scuppering Mr
Gloucester's designs, who, we learn in a truly malevolent
soliloquy, only married Necessity in order to get his hands on
her father's estate. Fleetingly, he contemplates killing his own
son – and, thus, reversing his father-in-law's remission –
however, pillow in hand, he cannot bring himself to do it.
But as his gambling debts mount (Necessity's handsome
dowry long since squandered, her father still enjoying rude
health) he is enjoined to take drastic action – and, while out
hunting with Wilkie, kills him in cold blood and maintains
that his death was a tragic accident. Somewhat implausibly,
the authorities take him at his word; Necessity, though, is
unconvinced. And, when Mr Gloucester takes charge of the
cotton mill – firing men, hiring children, imposing on the
workforce barbaric conditions and inhumane hours – she is
certain of his guilt. She appeals to the Dowdy Cleric, who,
after a lot of homiletic nonsense, promises to help; however,

the rapscallion betrays her, informing Mr Gloucester of her 'maniacal ravings' on the pretext that, ravaged by grief, she has temporarily taken leave of her senses. But despite the fact that Necessity has no concrete evidence, Mr Gloucester – in a shrewd pre-emptive strike calculated to undermine her credibility – applies for a parliamentary divorce on the grounds that his wife (doubtless due to her dementia) has been having 'criminal conversations' – i.e. sex – with a peripatetic tinker. The church court – in cahoots with the Dowdy Cleric – upholds Mr Gloucester's claim. Overnight, Necessity is a social outcast, spurned by gentry and common folk alike. And when at last the marriage is dissolved by parliament, Mr Gloucester is of course awarded custody of their son.

Six months later, Necessity – who, now penniless, has been forced to find work in a nearby village – gone berserk without her beloved Sebastien, steals a horse and gallops the two score miles to —field, where, pounding on Mr Gloucester's door, she demands, then beseeches, finally begs, to see her son. Mr Gloucester, exhausted after an especially abandoned night of revelry – during the course of which he routed all his servants from the house by dressing up as a ghoul – sleeps soundly throughout. Sebastien, though, bestirred by the sound of his mother's voice, rocks his crib so violently that he upsets a candle, kindling the conflagration that will kill his father and raze his house to the ground. Meanwhile, Necessity has ridden back to —ton, and only learns of the fire when the Dowdy Cleric writes to apprise her of Sebastien's death. In actuality, notwithstanding a nasty burn on his foot, he escaped unscathed. However, the

Dowdy Cleric, on the grounds that Necessity, given her divorce, is morally unsound and therefore incapable of caring for a child, entrusts Sebastien to Mr Gloucester's brother – a ne'er-do-well who, having sold the cotton mill, emigrates to Australia in order to escape Monty's bloodthirsty creditors.

Book Three opens with Necessity staring out of a casement window in the house in which she now works as a governess. Sixteen years have passed, and Necessity, at thirty-six, is in the full flower of her womanhood – however, she has been inconsolable since the death of her son, and therefore unamenable to the advances of her master, his batman, the coachman and sundry other lovestruck swains. She is staring at the new stable-boy, Dib. Her heart fairly overflows with pity at the sight of his disfiguring club foot. And yet his face seems Strangely Familiar. 'Why, he reminds me of Sebastien, my dear departed brother,' thinks Necessity. 'O Sebastien! if only you could see me now; reduced to the station of a governess: cleaving to a life shorn of happiness and hope; mine eyes fixed forever beyond the grave to that time when at last my soul be borne unto that lofty empyrean whither you and my darling son reside. O! "that the Everlasting had not fixed/ His canon 'gainst self-slaughter." Would that we three were together now!'

Of course, Dib is her darling son Sebastien. In a series of flashbacks we are privy to his wretched childhood in Perth. He is beaten by his uncle, bullied by his uncle's kids, ridiculed and reviled for his club foot – even his aunt turns out to be a termagant. His uncle, Sterling Supper, tells Dib that both his parents perished in a fire. His father, he learns, was a gambler and a sot; his mother, by all accounts, a twopenny-halfpenny whore. But Dib (a derogatory moniker that, unbeknownst to Sebastien, soon supplanted his real name) cannot bring himself to believe it: his mother, he knows in his heart of hearts, was a Good Woman. His uncle is obviously lying (although, if Sterling is any index, Dib's father probably was the bounder he described). Thus, aged eighteen, Dib sets out to find The Truth – and stows away aboard a cargo ship bound for England. Ferreted out by the ship's-mate, he is soundly flogged and treated like a slave for the rest of the journey. Hence by the time they dock at Southampton, Dib is in pretty poor shape and – destitute, exhausted, barely able to walk, let alone traverse the 200-odd miles to —field – begins to look for work. Finally, when Dib is on the brink of starvation, Necessity's master, moved by his plight, gives him a job in the stables.

Upon beholding Necessity, Dib, like most everyone she meets, is instantly smitten. 'Whenever she was near, Dib felt his breast empierced by happiness; his being ennobled and emparadised by hers. She was the loveliest, comeliest, most kind, charitable, warm-hearted and eligible creature he had ever met, or could ever have hoped to meet: indeed, in Dib's eyes she appeared more like a goddess than a mortal, a deathless Aphrodite as opposed to an earthly governess.' But what, wonders Dib dolefully, could someone like Necessity possibly see in a 'lameter' such as he? However, being high-born, he has inherited Necessity's excruciating beauty and his father's robust indefatigable frame. And Necessity, upon hearing Dib's harrowing story, falls irreversibly in love with him.

'What was your mother's name, child?' asked Necessity.

'I don't know, ma'am.'

'Please, call me Necessity, won't you?'

'Necessity,' said Dib, his cheeks afire with diffident rapture, his knees momently buckling as if beneath their burthen of joy. 'My uncle claims to have forgotten.'

'Why, that is scandalous: simply scandalous! – You poor child; you poor, poor child.'

She opened wide her arms; Dib threw himself against her, his heart athrill with untold ecstasies of passion: Necessity, quite overcome herself, clasped him swooning to her breast.

'I love you,' he ejaculated fiercely, his lambent blue eyes bedashed with tears. 'Miss Channing, forgive me: I love you!'

'Dearest Dib,' replied Necessity, weeping now herself, 'there is nothing to forgive: I love you, too. And, in the queerest way, I feel as if I had *always* loved you.'

Come the morning, Necessity takes leave of her master on the pretext of attending her father's funeral, and she and Dib sally forth to —field, to visit his mother's grave. Of course, Necessity is struck by the coincidence of both her son and Dib's mother dying in the same town, in the same circumstances and at approximately the same time; however, —field is a large town and fires are far from uncommon, and even though it crosses her mind that if her son hadn't died he'd be Dib's age now (there is after all a certain resemblance), his surname is Supper not Gloucester, and, moreover, she knows incontrovertibly that Sebastien is dead, she had visited his grave. And, it is darkly albeit circumspectly hinted, Dib is now her lover.

At —field cemetery, they vainly scour the headstones for a Mr and Mrs Montagu Supper. Necessity, not wishing to disclose her ill-starred past lest Dib think her a Fallen Woman, has heretofore kept silent about her son; now, however, face to face with his pathetically pint-sized grave, she can contain herself no more and, keening like a banshee, collapses in Dib's arms. At which point the Dowdy Cleric, who has been spying on them from the rectory, steps forward and malignantly tells all: interred in Sebastien's grave is a rabid mongrel. While tracing Mr Gloucester's nearest living relative he discovered that his real name was Supper (Gloucester being but one in a long list of *nom de guerres* assumed in order to frustrate his countless creditors). And, to persuade the reluctant Sterling to take charge of Sebastien, he told him that the infant's mother also expired in the fire.

'But why?' asked Necessity at last. 'Rector, answer me, why?'

'Revenge, sweet Necessity! Revenge! Who could have foretold that it would be so sweet. Estranged by half the earth and several oceans, mother and son are yet conjoined in that most unholy alliance: the Unspeakable Taboo!'

'Rector, forgive me; I am ignorant,' said Dib. 'I know not of what you speak.'

'Fool! do I have to underscore the obvious? You, Dib, are Sebastien, Necessity's son; Necessity is your mother; and, observing your amorous deportment from yonder rectory, I would opine your paramour withal! Am I wrong?'

'But, but . . .' said Necessity, stepping backwards.

"'Who more wretched, more afflicted now,/ With cruel misery, with fell disaster,/ Your life in dust and ashes?'"

The Dowdy Cleric gets no answer, for Necessity, repulsed by his derision, topples backwards into an open grave and is impaled on a pick. Slow Sebastien, belatedly grasping the enormity of the Dowdy Cleric's machinations, in a paroxysm of violent anguish and grief, puts out both his eyes. "'Unhappy your intention, and/ unhappy/ Your fate,'" says the Dowdy Cleric bitterly. "'Would that I had never known you!'"

23

In much the same spirit as one bravely resolves to see the dentist after numerous reminders, I arrange to meet my mother for lunch the following day.

The bar of the Regent, after the harsh spring sun, is comfortingly smoky and dim. The counter is of a blue-veined marble with a brass handrail, and extends the entire width of the room. Beyond, arrayed on backlit glass shelves, is a many-coloured, seemingly infinite selection of spirits, mixers and vermouths. My mother, perched before a Bloody Mary, is talking to the barman. Even though, next to her packet of Cartier, she has an expensive gold lighter, she haughtily waits for him to do the honours with his Bic, slyly caressing, as he does so, his right hand.

'Really, Gerard,' she says, gracefully exhaling, 'I simply can't *believe* you don't have a girlfriend. Handsome young man such as yourself.'

'Yes, sir,' he says, looking up.

'Chivas Regal. No ice.'

'Miff! *Dah*ling!' cries Theresa theatrically. 'Well don't just stand there, give a kiss.' Although it is she who stands, throws her arms around me and half squeezes me to death.

'Hi, *Mom*,' I say sarcastically.

'*Ssh*. Gerard'll hear,' she whispers in my ear. Then, abruptly releasing me: 'And you can mix me another Bloody Mary, Gerard. Have someone send them over.'

Theresa leads me to one of the lamplit leather booths bordering the bar. She is wearing a tight, black, inappropriately *decolleté* dress, doubtless the work of some modish designer – Versace? Yves Saint Laurent? – that somehow contrives to make her breasts appear larger, plumper than I recall. At forty-two she is still unquestionably beautiful, with her opulent red hair and amber eyes; but when she reaches across the table to take my hand, her once lucent skin seems drawn, artificial, robbed of its satiny aspect.

'Miff, I must say, you're looking terrifically handsome. Don't tell me you've gone and got yourself a girlfriend at last.'

Withdrawing my hand to light a cigarette, I say: 'I don't really think that's any of your business.'

'Really, Miff, I am your mother after all. I mean isn't that what mothers do? Vetting girlfriends, that sort of thing?'

'I wouldn't know. I've never had a proper mother.'

'Darling, you are being beastly. I mean it's not as if . . .'

A waiter arrives with the drinks; as he turns to leave, Theresa says: 'And oh, get Gerard to send over a decent bottle of Christal.'

'Gerard?' says the waiter, feigning incomprehension.

'*Gerard*. The *bar*man,' as if talking to an idiot.

'The barman's name, madam, is Jeremy.'

'*And your point is?*' Then, with a disdainful shooing motion: 'Run along now.' And, as he leaves: 'Really, the service in this country is *disgraceful*. In Palm Beach –'

'How is Bernie?' I ask, cutting short the inevitable tirade.

'How should I know? I haven't seen him since the divorce.'

'*Divorce?* You didn't tell me.'

'The little shit. Can you believe it, I had to settle for a *measly* three million. He went and hired this celebrity divorce lawyer. And then I'd signed this pre*pos*terous prenuptial agreement –'

'Three *million*,' I say, as the sum sinks in.

'Outrageous, isn't it?'

'I was going to say that's an awful lot.'

'Like hell it is. He's worth at least a hundred. He probably paid his lawyer more than he paid me.'

'So what happened?'

'Happened?'

'The divorce,' I say, lighting her cigarette.

'Oh, that. Bloody Bernie. Farcical, really. No, make that

63

trite. First, he pays for my facelift. Then he runs off with the plastic surgeon's secretary.'

'*Face*lift?'

'You mean you didn't notice?' Then, when I don't answer: 'You haven't even noticed my new boobs.'

'You mean those are implants?'

'Magnificent, aren't they?'

A scalloped margin of bra – lacy, white – shows beneath the black of her dress. 'Stunning,' I reply – God help me – truthfully.

Theresa smiles at me coyly. 'Sweet of you to say.'

Averting my gaze from her voluptuous cleavage, I knock back my Scotch. 'Did Bernie buy those for you, too?'

'No, I paid for them myself. Thought they might boost my morale.'

The champagne arrives; with stony ceremony, is presented and poured.

'Really, the whole thing was *too* humiliating.'

'The operation?'

'No, you idiot, the divorce. Bernie. I mean I wouldn't have minded if he'd had an affair. *Affairs* I can live with. But this Didi woman – what am I talking about, she's only nineteen – said she wouldn't sleep with him unless they were married. Pretended she was a *virgin* – the little slut's probably *fucked* half of Palm Beach. And then Bernie wanted kids – even though he's got *four* from previous marriages. The megalomaniac. And . . . you know. After Sarah . . .' Then, as I look away: 'But enough about me. Tell me about you. You're living with your *grand*ma, of all people.'

'Yes.'

'But what on earth for?'

'Oh, you know. Dad . . .' is all I can say.

'Only too well.' Then: 'Darling, where are your manners? Can't you *see* my glass is empty?'

'We're not on a *date*,' I say petulantly. 'Anyway, I thought we were going to have lunch.'

'Oh bugger that. Haven't you heard food's *fattening?*' Then, as I begrudgingly pour the champagne: 'So. What've you been doing with yourself?'

'Working.'

'Oh, a *job*. Really? What is it that you "do"?'

'I work in a bookshop.'

'A *book*shop?' as if I'd said a brothel.

'What's wrong with that?'

'Well, it's not very *exalted*, is it? I mean what am I sup*posed* to tell my friends?'

'Tell them I'm a drug addict. Tell them I'm a pimp. Tell them I mastermind armed robberies.'

'Well, it's certainly more flam*boyant* than selling books. Speaking of which, weren't *you* working on a book or something?'

'I'm writing a novel.'

'Well isn't it finished yet?'

'No. Contrary to popular opinion, it takes rather longer to write a book than it does to read it.'

'You should speak to my agent.'

'*You*,' incredulously, 'have an agent? What for?'

'Didn't I tell you? I've got a book coming out in the fall.'

God, I think, *not Theresa too*! Who next? Our waiter, the doorman, one of the chambermaids? 'What kind of a book?' I ask sceptically.

'It's a memoir of my marriage to Bernie. It's called *In Bed with the Butterball King: An Intimate Portrait of Bernie McClintock.*'

'And you *wrote* it?'

'Of course not. Somebody else did, silly. But my name's on the front. And, what's more, Simon & Schuster paid $200,000 for the privilege.'

'But *why*? I mean, who *gives* a shit about Bernie McClintock? I know I don't – and you were married to him.'

'Darling, if you're rich, the American public wants to know what time of the day you defecate. And, if you're very rich,' she continues acidly, 'they'll want to see photos of your shit.'

After our second bottle of champagne, we start drinking cocktails. Highballs for her. Whisky sours for me. By now we are both indisputably drunk. And Theresa, as is her wont, has lapsed into soliloquy.

'You know I'm glad I divorced Bernie,' she is saying. 'Really, he was hopeless in bed. Even after his penis extension. Don't know why he bothered. Couldn't have sex for three months. Not, of course, that I wanted to – with him. And then I could never tell the difference anyway. Although when he first got it done it swelled up to the size of a Coke can. Poor man, it was all he could do to *pee*. And, to give him credit, he was a veritable *stud* in comparison to your father. Really, Eric was awful. Hadn't a clue. You know I was the first person he slept with?'

'Christ, Theresa. I don't want to know,' I say – although, in actuality, I'm grimly intrigued.

'In retrospect,' she persists, oblivious to my protests, 'it was a miracle you were even con*ceived*. My God – what a mistake! Eric, dear, not you ... Although at the *time* he seemed like a pretty good bet. His father made good money. His mother had family money. When I saw their house – well, you can imagine how I felt. Or maybe you can't. I don't suppose you remember visiting your grandparents in Staines – that con*temptible* little hovel they used to call a house. If it wasn't for that boarding school, my scholarship, that window on a better world ... I dread to think. I'd probably be a receptionist in a doctor's surgery, a grubby teller in a bank. Living in some benighted little bungalow with a husband called Ted. I can't imagine anything worse – really, I'd prefer to be dead.' She knocks back her highball – and, catching the waiter's eye, signals for another. 'And then Eric was terribly sweet. Handsome, too, in his own way. We met at a party in Russell Square. Don't know *how* I ended up there. In those days all I *did* was party – all the bohos I hung around with then thought they were making some *profound* political statement by smoking pot. Or taking acid. As if substance abuse could somehow bring about a better world. Of course, I knew better. I knew what poverty was. The shame of second-hand clothes and penny pinching – the obsession with what you don't have. God, how I detested their psychedelic socialism – as if *they'd* ever wanted for anything. I'd have killed for their upbringing, their breeding, their *wealth* – all the things they pretended to despise. Which was why Eric was such a breath of fresh air – he never pretended to be a revolutionary or an anarchist or that his paintings would somehow set the world to rights. And the fact that he *was* so square, that he didn't take drugs, that he still believed in chivalry – that a man should pay for a woman and treat her with respect – was terrifically endearing. Back then when monogamy and marriage were seen as fascist institutions – 'stalwarts of the *status quo*', or some such rot. When fucking around was seen as a glorious affirmation of Free Love. And in the midst of this so-called revolution there was Eric, bless him, doing his PhD.'

She talks about my father's courtship. Old boyfriends. Trysts on Old Compton Street. The Coach and Horses. Soho in the seventies. The endless round of restaurants, cafés, bars. She talks about divorce. Her second husband. Living in America. Monaco. Paris. Milan. Her affairs. Staines. Her shitty childhood. She tells me she loves me. That she's always loved me. That she wishes things had been different. That she always wanted me to have the best.

Finally – drunk, talked-out – Theresa announces she needs to lie down. Riding up in the lift, dolefully reflecting on our relationship, I cannot help pining for a normal mum. An ordinary, unglamorous mum. She can be fat, ugly, embarrassing – just so long as she is there. A mum who irons my clothes, wears her hair in curlers and nags me to tidy my room. All of a sudden the banal stuff of family life – communal meals, Sunday walks, clannish get-togethers, naff holidays, supermarket shopping, charades, Cluedo, Trivial Pursuit – seem hopelessly cosy and desirable; however, unless I start a family of my own, in this life I'll never know them.

Theresa's is a sumptuous suite: lofty ceilings, cascading

cornices, an oversized bed, elegant Georgian furniture. From her balcony she commands a panoramic view of Regent's Park. Emerging from the bathroom, Theresa kicks off her shoes and sits on the edge of the bed.

'I, uh . . . I'll get going then.'

'No *stay*,' she says. 'You can help me with my dress.'

She stands and walks towards me; proffers me her back. As I obediently unzip her dress, I cannot help but inhale the trapped perfume of her warm milk-white flesh. She turns around, and, holding my gaze, unhooks her shoulder-straps and steps out of her dress. I am shocked and reluctantly aroused by my mother's whorish underwear: suspenders, girdle, white silk stockings and scant, all but transparent, panties. Her substantial upswung breasts are barely undergirt by a squiggly white brassière; the tops of both nipples slightly, tantalisingly obtrude.

'Fuck.'

'They *are* impressive, aren't they?' she says, cupping them in her hands.

Impetuously, she reaches behind her back and unclips her bra; staring transfixedly at her unencumbered breasts, her pale uptilting teats, I experience the first thick stirrings of lust, feel myself, in spite of everything, stiffen. She places my right hand on her left breast. I massage her bosom. She steps forward, and, swooping up on tiptoe, thrusts her tongue into my mouth. Automatically, as if to catch her, my arm encircles her waist, and, staggering backwards, we collapse on the bed. Sitting astride me, Theresa kisses me – wetly, aggressively – her heavy tits squashed against my chest. She yanks at my tie. Rips open my shirt: kisses my belly. My hard-on is crushed between her breasts. She unzips my trousers, frees my prick, and, as her mouth approaches, my dreamy impassivity suddenly gives way to vertiginous horror and disgust. 'No,' I say, pushing her aside. '*No*. Christ, I . . . What the fuck were you going to do?' 'I don't know,' she says, looking away. 'I don't know.'

24

The following evening at work, still feeling shellshocked, I console myself by talking to Kay. Kay, who, despite being several years my senior, inspires in me fatherly feelings of solicitude and love. Yes, gawky, pale, coltish Kay, with her straight, slightly russety, shoulder-length hair is, in many ways, my dream daughter. Indeed, part of her charm is her angelic androgeny – her banal, oddly comforting chitchat. We talk about the weather, Cynthia, children's books. The respective merits of The Famous Five and The Secret Seven. And, more often than not, her (only, younger) sister – who, as far as Kay is concerned, has it all: brains, beauty, a lucrative job, the biggest bedroom in their Islington flat (although, as Kay is quick to point out, Beth pays the lion's share of the rent and is therefore entitled to the airier boudoir).

'I mean it's not that I don't think she's wonderful, she is,' Kay is saying. 'It's just sometimes – oh, I don't know – I feel like such a failure in comparison.'

I am sitting downstairs at the Information Desk. Kay is supposed to be putting out books.

'Nonsense,' I say. 'Of course you're not a failure. You're the only published author in the shop.'

'*Oh, I know*, I shouldn't complain. It's just . . .'

'What, Kay? What?' I ask earnestly.

'She's so glamorous. So beautiful. Miff, if you met her you'd fall in love with her. I just know you would. Men do.'

'Not *all* men, surely?'

'I suppose' – she continues – 'I know it's an awful thing to say, but I suppose I'm just jealous.'

'But Kay you're lovely. There's no reason to be jealous.'

'Oh,' kneading her hands together, 'you're just saying that.'

'I am *not*,' I expostulate.

Blushing deeply, staring at the floor, she says: 'I . . . think you're lovely, too.' Then, recovering herself: 'But it's not just her beauty. She's . . . brilliant.'

'At what?'

'Everything. At her job.'

'What does she do again?'

'She's a copywriter at Olgilvy and Mather.'

'O&M,' butts in Steve, coming down the stairs. 'Good agency.'

'One of the best,' says Kay with palpable pride.

'But, Kay, you can write children's books. Anyone can write ads.'

'The hell they can,' says Steve, a staunch proponent of pop culture. 'If Shakespeare were alive today, he'd be writing ads.'

'Have you *read Hamlet?*'

'No. Seriously. Copywriters are the bards of the twentieth century. The true chroniclers of our post-postmodern age.'

'Oh that's such a lot of shit,' I say angrily, although ordinarily I'm careful not to swear in front of Kay.

'Miff, you're out of date, man. You're still living in the dark ages.'

'And you're living up your own arsehole. I'm sorry, but *ads* are not art. They're contemptible. *Cretinising.* They've engendered a generation of fuckwits with the attention span of a small fart.'

Slightly rattled, Steve says: 'Yeah, well, say what you like, but I'd rather watch ads than read Proust.'

'Christ, Steve, how can you *say* that? If you think adverts are so fucking great you should go get a job in the goddamn industry.'

'I tried,' he confesses sheepishly. 'I didn't get in.'

'So you wrote a novel *instead?* Is *that* what you're saying?'

'Uh, yeah.'

'What's going on?' asks Patricia – or, as she likes to be called, P – our deputy manageress.

'Nothing,' Steve and I reply in tandem (Kay, sensing danger, has already fled).

'You *boys*,' she says coquettishly. Then: 'Mine's a coffee, thanks, Steve.'

'Ye*ssum*, Missus P,' parodying a plantation slave. 'Al'll do it *kind*ly and *glad*ly.'

'Oi, *watch* it,' she says. And, as he leaves, gently pats him on the rump.

Patricia is of the opinion that she's all but irresistible – with her mousy-brown bangs, her ruddy farm-girl's face, her robust belovehandled body; which, I suppose, is another way of saying she'll sleep with anyone: okay, not *any*one, although rumour has it that she's slept with almost everyone – or, at least, more than half the men who've worked under her.

'So, Miff' – grazing my stubble – 'why haven't you shaved?'

'I just did. That there's a three-minute growth.'

'Tcha! Such a kidder,' she says girlishly. Then, with shocking stomach-turning salacity: 'You're so *butch*.'

'So, Peepee,' I say trying to change the subject. 'What's the scuttlebutt?'

'You what?'

'You know – the rumour, the goss.'

'Oh *that*. Well, let's see . . .' hooking a spray of hair behind her ear. 'Have you heard about Howard?'

'Howard?'

'The *new assistant manager*. God, Miff, where've you been?'

'Oh, yes, I know the fellow.'

'Well *apparently* he was involved in this love triangle at Charing Cross Road.'

'No *way*. He looks so humble.'

'Well, get this: He started a fight at the Pitcher and Piano with this guy Kevin – who *I* was briefly involved with – he was crap in bed – over this girl Trudy, who works at Fenchurch Street, who used to go out with Steve . . .'

What follows is an impossibly tangled skein of intrigue, that – given my, at best, patchy knowledge of Book Shop employees – is largely lost on me.

Presently, Victoria, looking quietly triumphant, comes to my rescue.

'Miff, your break,' she says haughtily.

'*Oh*,' says Patricia, who regards all female colleagues as competition, '*lah-de-da*.'

Victoria, though, is fairly entitled to her hauteur. On the strength of her heartfelt reading the other night, Poetaster – Outlandish's poetry imprint – have expressed an interest in her work. That said, Poetaster hardly enjoy the prestige of, say, Faber & Faber. Their leading light, Roberto Nonce, has so far produced five volumes on the subject of being dumped by his girlfriend. The first volume, *Absence*, is by far and away the strongest. The eponymous poem (reproduced here) is a fair example of his work.

your smell on my sheets
   your books on my shelf
      those panties I refuse to wash

your hair on my pillow
   those photos we took
      the love we made in my bath

you say you want your records back
   bitch, I want back my life
      buy your own fucking records, I say

you said
   you'd be
      my wife

The next three volumes (*Lucyless in Gaza, Without Her*, and *I Want You Back!*) are all inferior variations on the first, inexorably leading to the last bathetic volume, *I Love Lucy*, which, in spite of its awfulness, none the less inspires a certain concern for the author's sanity.

25

Entering the staffroom, I find Clare intent on a book of photography.

'Clare!' I say, always pleased to see her. ,

'A' right, Miff.'

'What've you got there?'

'*Ah*, it's *great*. It's called *Naked* by Elizabetta van der Van. She spent an entire year exposin' 'erself to people in public – parks an' supermarkets, places like that. The book's a photographic record of people's reactions to 'er naked body. 'Ere,' handing me the book, 'look.'

The front cover shows Ms van der Van exposing herself in a greasy raincoat. 'Nice tits,' I say.

'*Ah*, Miff! Yer such a *perv*.'

Inside there are men, women and children, exhibiting more or less the same response: surprise tempered with incipient amusement (men) or wonder (women and children). In one photo she has even contrived to flash at a flasher as he (a wild-eyed octogenarian) flashes at her. What might've been (marginally) more interesting would have been to have take the photo not at the exact instant of exposure but a few seconds later – however, this seems not to've occurred to Elizabetta, who, one concludes, was far more concerned with getting her tits out than with, as the backflap has it, 'examining society's ambiguous attitude to nakedness'.

'They're great, aren't they?'

'Interesting,' I say. 'But . . . I don't understand. How did she manage to take photographs *while* she was exposing herself?'

'Ah, that's what so brilliant. She designed a miniature camera that'd fit inside a pair of dark glasses – which were wired up to a remote device she 'id in 'er pocket.'

'I see.'

'It's all there in the introduction,' she says, pointing at the book. Then, pouring the remainder of her coffee in the sink: 'I'll see you out there.'

After making myself a tea, I settle down to Elizabetta's preface.

'In *Naked*,' she writes, 'I wanted to explore the English attitude to nakedness. Since Victorian times nakedness, as opposed to nudity, has been the province of pornography. Even amid our most radical feminists the female body still bears the stigmata of shame. Already I can hear their indignant dissent: *Elizabetta, you are wrong!* But why else would they denounce the benign, frequently beautiful female nudity in both sculpture and fine art as derogatory and exploitative? Even in the ancient world, as embodied in the unhappy fate of Actaeon, female nakedness was taboo.

'Looking back, the most crushing moment of my childhood was when my mother told me it was no longer permissible to run around naked. Nice girls, she told me, cover themselves up . . .'

'Miff!' says Phil, coming into the staffroom. 'There too art.'

'Philippe! Salut!'

'Saloo-to-you-too.'

Phil is wearing a tight short-sleeved shirt with a vermilion cravat.

'Alors, Philippe,' I say, 'ca te plairait de coucher avec moi?'

'Je coucher, Miff, dans le nod.'

'Tu sais que je coucher avec ta mère?'

'May mon mare coucher dans les *peejamais*.' Then: 'Why d'you ask?'

'Oh, no reason.'

'Now, what I wanted to *say* to you *was*: Are you coming to my show?'

'What show?'

Phil explains that he and a group of like-minded avant-gardists are disdaining to exhibit their work alongside that of their fellow – presumably, less radical – students at Central St Martin's, and are holding an exhibition of their own.

'Oh, I see,' I say. 'So you're the rebel Impressionists putting on a rival show, and St Martin's are the Salon.'

'May we,' says Phil. Then: 'But what's all this about a salon?'

26

In the travel section I find Judy talking to Steve.

'Ooh, it was dead romantic.'

'What was?' I ask.

'Her date with Nutter,' says Steve.

'So he went through with it?'

'And then some,' says Judy. 'He bought me a dozen red roses. I took his arm. We dined at Criterion Marco Pierre White.'

'Bullshit,' says Steve.

'What colour are his eyes?' I ask.

'What was his mother's maiden name?'

'Ooh, um . . .'

I begin to whistle 'The Mountains of Morne'.

'What colour were his socks?' says Steve, taking up the tune, which we proceed to whistle in relay.

'Why, did you kill him?'

'You killed him, didn't you?'

'You've made the whole thing up.'

'When was the last time you read *The Communist Manifesto*?'

'How many stanzas in *The Faerie Queen*?'

'Stop it! Stop it!' says Judy. Then, taking a deep breath: 'Brown. Blesset. Blue with red polkadots. I didn't. I didn't. I haven't, and how dare you. Eighteen. I don't know.'

'So, are you going to see him again?' I say.

'For sure.'

Steve, lying prone on the ground, says: 'We picked violets in April, Mother and I. Violets. Violates. Violence.' Then: 'Chilly here, isn't it?'

27

I awaken to the sounds of Clare billing up: the rustle of Rizzla and tobacco; the pungent smell of burnt hashish. She is sitting crosslegged on the mattress beside me. As usual, in the pitiless morning light, I am repulsed by the sight of her body: her pale oily skin, her drooping tits, the pronounced rolls of flab around her midriff. My mouth is acrid with cheap whisky and dope; I feel hot and fetid. The floor is strewn with records and tapes, soiled clothes, rank underwear, empty bottles and mugs, Coke cans ringed with fag ash, week-old packets of Drum . . . But however tremendous my remorse, however desperate the squalor, however close the queasy stench of stale debauchery, I none the less have an erection. 'Hey,' I say, lightly touching Clare's back, a minefield of palatinate pimples. 'Mornin',' she says, tamping down the tobacco with the removable flint-end of her Clipper. Taking her right hand – on which there are encrypted numerous reminders and notes – I burrow beneath the duvet and place it on my prick. Setting her joint to one side, Clare calmly strips back the covers, straddles me on her knees, and, with her back still towards me, begins to ease herself on to my dick. Her cunt, ordinarily so wet and oleaginous, is dry. After several, for me painful, attempts, each time probing just a little bit further until it feels as though my foreskin will surely snap, our juices start to flow and I slide into her. Fearing for my erection, I close my eyes on her jouncing haunches, her greasy back; concentrate on our erratic rhythm. Blindly, I grab hold of her hips: pull her down, push her up. Pull her down. Push her up. Finally, squander my weary seed inside her . . .

28

'So,' says Clare, lighting up her spliff, ''ow's Iseult?'

'Fine,' I say. Then: 'Actually, if you want to know the truth, she's fucking nuts.'

'Why, what's she done?'

'Here' – rummaging through my trousers for Iseult's note from the previous night – 'read this'.

'"Miff. Please bring Naughty Boy by on Saturday at 2 pm. His mummy loves him dearly. – I."'

'You see what I mean?' I say, refusing Clare's spliff.

'Who the fuck's Naughty Boy?' After I tell her, she says: 'Flippin 'eck. I wonder what Freud would've made of Iseult.'

'Oh fuck Freud. He'd have said she had an inverse Oedipus Complex, arising from incompletely suppressed infantile sexual longings, compounded by – fuck knows – some catalysing childhood trauma. Which, at bottom, doesn't really tell me anything.'

'Miff, I sense yer un'appy.'

'Of course I'm fucking unhappy.'

'Well why d'yer do it then?'

'Because . . . I don't know. Because I'm in love with her.'

'An d'yer think she loves yer?'

'In a nappy, sure. When I'm her darling Naughty Boy. But as soon as I put my clothes on, it's like . . . I don't exist. At the shop it's unbearable. She completely ignores me. Refuses to speak to me. I . . .' Then, spying a pair of rumpled underpants. 'Whose are those?'

'What?'

'*Those*,' I say, gesturing with my foot, 'those *pants.*'

'Oh, Steve's. 'E must've left 'em 'ere on Wednesday.'

'*Steve's*?' incredulously. 'What was *Steve* doing here?'

'What d'yer think?'

'You mean to tell me you've been fucking *Steve*?'

'What's wrong with that? Yer've been shaggin' Iseult.'

But, I want to say, *that's different.*

'I thought,' she says, taking rapid tokes from the now minuscule spliff, 'yer knew.'

'No.' Then: 'Anyway, how could Steve forget his underwear? I mean, it's not one of those things one forgets.'

''E must've taken mine.'

'*What?* You mean to tell me he's been wearing your . . . *knickers?*'

'So what? I've worn 'is Y-fronts before.'

'So I could've spoken to him while he was wearing them!'

'God, Miff, for a man who wears nappies you ain't 'alf a prude.'

'Christ. You think you know someone. Then . . .'

'What?'

'Nothing. Steve's a nice guy.'

'Steve's great.'

'So what's he like? What's,' pausing dramatically, 'the

"real" Steve like?'

'Actually, 'e's dead romantic. It was a side of 'im I 'adn't suspected till we shagged. Then when I read 'is novel –'

'No way! You've actually *read* it? *The Death of Love?* The epic 1000-page masterpiece? *The* post-postmodern novel?'

'Yup.'

'So what's it like? What's it about? I'd have thought it'd be unreadable.'

'Basically, from what I can tell, it's about this creative genius called Steve who 'as an affair with an English supermodel by the name of Kate Boss. Then when they split up 'e writes this ginormous novel about their affair in an attempt to win 'er back. But the publishers all reject 'im because they fail to recognise 'is radical genius, an' Kate starts going out with this famous actor by the name of Johnny Nepp. After that 'e goes off 'is nut. Starts doin' in all these editors. If yer ask me, it's a mess.'

'But what about all that nonsense with Derrida and Foucault?'

'Who?'

'They're French philosophers.'

'Well if they're in it I don't remember. I only read the forty-ninth draft.'

'Christ, how many drafts has he written?'

'I don't know. To tell the truth' – starting to get dressed – 'I didn't read it very carefully. The language ... I can't describe it. It's like: In the charnel 'ouse of my creative unconscious I roam supreme. Godlike, I banish the phantoms of a decrepit civilisation. It goes on like that for ever. The affair itself is dealt with in the first fifty pages. An' the rest of it

is all 'im writin' 'is bleedin' book an' gettin' rejected an' doin'
in editors.' Then, clambering into a tepeelike rainbow-hued
sweater: 'D'yer wanna cup of tea?'

'I'd love one. Thanks.'

29

Some minutes later, now fully dressed, I bump into Kirsty
(one of Clare's flatmates, or at least one of a handful of people
who habitually doss on the floor) and a man I've never met
before doing bong hits in the kitchen.

'Hey, man. Whose is the wine?' says the latter, squinting
into the neck of a half-drunk bottle of BudJet Red.

'I don't know. But I think it's fairly ancient,' I reply,
gesturing at the innumerable empties arrayed on the table,
sideboard and floor. Then, turning to Kirsty: 'Where's
Clare?'

Kirsty, who has just taken an almighty hit, raises her hand
and screws up her eyes as if besieged by constipation.
Meanwhile, the man (her boyfriend?) has upended the bottle
of wine: suddenly puzzled, he pauses, removes a dead
matchstick from his mouth, and, shrugging his shoulders,
swallows. 'Try the bog,' says Kirsty, finally exhaling.

Outside the door to the toilet, I hear the thoughtful
clicking of a camera. 'Come in,' says Clare after I knock.

Opening the door I am greeted by a warm fecal odour.
Clare, standing athwart the toilet bowl, is taking photos with
her beat-up 20mm Pentax. 'Clare. What're you doing?' I say,

utterly aghast.

'It's for a new project I'm doin' on waste. I got the idea while I was shootin' all that rubbish for me project on chaos. What makes waste waste? What gives it its identity? 'Ow does it manifest itself in our lives? Then, while I was takin' a dump, I got to thinkin' about the shameful nature of 'uman waste. An' why should that be? I'm 'opin' that by takin' photos I can somehow objectify it – force people to look afresh at it without feelin' sick or ashamed. – What d'yer think?'

'Interesting,' I say.

30

Outside, the sky is streaked with cirrus, the sun's warmth dissipated by a frigid wind. As usual, walking along Pentonville Road, I feel imperiled by my jacket and tie. Even in daylight I half-expect to be set upon by some desperate crack-fiend; mugged by dint of appearing out of place. I do my best to ignore the jittery whores; the plastic bags of soiled belongings; the dealers, the beggars and their laconic cardboard plaques ('HUNGRY. HOMELESS'); the mephitic alleys of piss and puke and come, the empty cans of Tennent's Super; the KostKutters, the kebab shops, the amusement arcades. Once inside the station, I buy a travelcard and take the Piccadilly Line to South Ken. Emerging from the Underground into the cosmopolitan clamour of the Old Brompton Road, with its restaurants and coffee shops, its boutiques, bookstores and bars, the international newsagents boasting copies of the *Herald Tribune* and *Le Monde*, I feel confident in my colouration, if anything dowdy in my non-designer garb. Back at my gran's, I take a shower – squeamishly scrub away the smegma that stinks so keenly of Clare – and change into fresh clothes: black jacket, black jeans, a cream turtle-neck, a high-breasted navy-blue waistcoat. After stopping off to buy a copy of the *TLS* and a pack of Chesterfields, feeling expansive I decide to brunch at Café Rouge. Since I abandoned my novel back in December, I have been feeling terribly listless and indolent during the day; and, despite my horror of mindless drudgery, the besuited automata one encounters in rush-hour tubes, my liberty still leaves me feeling somewhat guilty, like a Chekhov character – a Chebutykin or an Uncle Vanya – gone to seed with too much sloth. At least when I was writing, albeit dismally, I could claim to be a writer; now, however, with nothing to do, I am devoid of an identity. I spend my days in art-house cinemas (the Metro, the Lumière, the ICA), galleries (the RA, the Tate, the National) – the British and Natural History museums. I suppose, at bottom, I'm always hoping for a brief encounter – or, rather, I'm always searching for my wife. For wouldn't it be apt if we met in an art gallery? Collided in a cinema aisle? Friends will ask us how we met: *Actually, it was quite amusing. I was in the Tate looking at a portrait by John Singer Sargent when . . . I'd just seen* Cyclo *at the Swiss Centre when who should I – literally – bump into but . . .* And while I sincerely doubt that it'll ever happen, it's nice to think that these things still can and do. I remind myself that what's important here is my cultural edification. After all, I'm not so far gone on the path to poetic lonesomeness that I cease to look at the pictures or to watch the film or to gaze at the Aztec artifacts, Etruscan earthenware etc., with due wonderment and awe. It's more that, at the back of my mind, there shines, willy-nilly, the pilot-light of romantic possibility, the tremulous promise of true love . . . After a couple of croissants and a double espresso, I stroll down Gloucester Road and enter Hyde Park. To my right and left there are parterres of exotic trees and shrubbery – home to half a dozen tumbling grey squirrels. The benches are mostly occupied by pensioners, the odd ageing queen, a fat spinster with a thermos of tea, several sticky pastries and a bumper crossword book. Beyond, in among the omnipresent plane trees, I see three dogs trying to fuck, their exasperated owners, gardeners, young mothers, emphatically ugly English kids. On Rotten Row, despite the sundry piles of horse-shit, there is only one horse. Still, it appears to me a mythic beast – at once fearsome and beautiful, elegant, enormous, only partially tamed. And what dignity when compared to the pullulating joggers – with their swearing and their spitting and their sweat-soaked clothes – looking less like athletes than so many sex offenders fleeing from the law. Taking the underpass at Hyde Park Corner, I cross over into Green Park and fairly march up Constitution Hill, feeling, amid a coachful of recently debouched Italian tourists, oddly, exaltedly, British. And, gazing at the sentries outside Buckingham Palace, with their trim uniforms and preposterous furry hats pulled low on their foreheads, lending their otherwise martial visages a look of irremediable stupidity, one senses just how alien we must appear to the assembled, duly dumbstruck foreigners. On, then, to the Mall, with its pretty reddish-pink asphalt, St James's Park to my right, the squat ground-floor Doric columns of Carlton House Terrace on my left. By now the clouds have all but evaporated, laying bare a stark crystalline sky of unabated blue; the wind, still gusty and gelid, bellies the back of my jacket, plays havoc with my hair. On an impulse I enter the ICA, browse in the bookshop, and, finally, pay one pound fifty just to get in to the goddamn bar. As always, at least at lunchtime, it is filled with suits and a handful of would-be bohemians. I buy a pint of Red Stripe and sit in a window-seat. At the table next to me are a youngish couple holding hands. They are so wrapped up in one another they seem utterly insensible to their surroundings – the clatter and the laughter and the smoke. 'Darling,' he says, 'really.' 'Oh, just ignore me,' she replies. 'I'm being silly.' Then, in a whisper: 'I want to suck your willy.' Sick with envy, I attempt to read my *TLS*. But my thoughts are elsewhere. Iseult. Clare. Theresa. When I was younger, I wanted nothing better than to be a devoted husband. How easy it had seemed to me then. One grew up. One went out with women. Then, one fine day, one met one's wife. Just like that. What could be easier than falling in love? Yes, I wanted to be a Family Man. I wanted a wife and a house and a couple of kids. Christ, I *still* hanker after a garage cluttered with junk. All the flotsam – old tennis rackets, ancient sneakers, bikes, snorkels, ping pong bats – of family life. On Sundays I'll wake up early and mow the lawn. Maybe I'll wash the car. Tinker with some faulty domestic appliance. I'll be one of those dads who fancy themselves as a handy man. I'll have to fuck up the plumbing good and proper before I call a professional in. I'll have to take the toaster to bits before I capitulate and buy a new one. Hell, I'll even chum up to the mechanic who fixes my car – pretend I know what I'm talking about. *The carburettor, you say*, I'll say, nodding sagely. *Yes, I thought it was . . .* the transmission, the clutch, the brakes . . . But can I take romantic walks with Iseult through St James's Park? Can I enjoy a candlelit diner with Clare at an expensive restaurant? – while she takes photos of her shit in the bogs. Can I marry my own mother? *Your Honour, I'd like to call as my first witness, Oedipus the King. Mr Rex, wouldn't it be correct to say that you and Jocasta enjoyed* carnal *relations?* And how, if I'm to support a family, will I win the proverbial bread? My novel still sulks in a locked desk drawer – deformed, unfinished . . . scarce half made up. Will I, too, eventually renounce my ambition and write about the Death of the Novel in the *TLS?* Or worse: awake one morning from uneasy dreams to find myself transformed into a grotesque full-timer? I dread to think.

31

'What does "algedonic" mean?' asks Anthony later that afternoon.

I tell him to look it up in the dictionary.

'I did. It wasn't there.'

'Loosely, it means pertaining to pleasure and pain.'

'How d'you know?' he says resentfully.

'Because I looked it up when *I* read *The Magus.*'

'Where?'

'Here,' I say, handing him my *Shorter OED*.

'Well then why,' he says, having read the definition, 'didn't he say so?'

'Christ, Anthony. It's like saying why use the word "car" when you can say "four-wheeled vehicle used for the conveyance of passengers and their luggage" instead.'

'No it's not.'

'Yes it *is*. You've got to stop trying to make a virtue of your ignorance. I know it's hard, but if you look up every word you don't understand then pretty soon you'll have a decent-sized vocabulary and you won't have to feel so epically frustrated every time you read a novel.'

'Terry Pratchett doesn't use words I don't understand.'

'Terry Pratchett! There *is* no Terry Pratchett. It's a computer programme that spews out books.'

'Well what makes John Fowles so good?'

'Everything. His stylistic brilliance. His sensitivity to art, literature, history, nature. The reach and ambition of his plots.'

'Pah,' snorts Anthony, biting his nail.

'And what's that supposed to mean?'

'Well, the plot – it didn't make sense.'

'Why not?'

'Nicholas and Alison. I mean I loved that bit at the beginning – you know, when they're falling in love. And all they do is have sex and drink wine and make love. I mean, it all seemed so perfect. Then . . . then he sods off to Greece. Why?'

'Well, for one thing, she's half-Australian. And, as Nicholas remarks to Julie later on, Australians tend to be rather "culturally half-baked".'

'So?'

'So young Nicholas is a bit of a snob. In a terribly English way, he's embarrassed by what he sees as her vulgarity – whilst simultaneously despising the English bourgeoisie for their petty snobbery. And then he's repulsed by the spectacle of Alison's love, cannot countenance commitment, and rather suspects that he might do better elsewhere – i.e. Julie. Remember, this is the man who when his parents died felt a *faux* existential rush of freedom.'

'If *I* was Nicholas I'd have married her,' he says chivalrously. Then: 'And then why does he go for *Julie?* I had my suspicions about her from the start.'

'She's cultured. She's English. She's ravishingly beautiful. And, perhaps more importantly, she's practically a virgin.'

'So?'

'It's the classic distinction. Alison's the whore. Julie's the virgin.' Anthony still looks perplexed. 'Okay. When he's fucking Alison he's worrying about all the other men she's slept with – and the size of his cock. And more than once in the novel he says something along the lines of: Look, I know I'm a cop-out in bed. And can't quite believe it when Alison says he's not – and anyway it doesn't matter. Whereas with Julie the only person he's got to worry about is her former fiancé – who, being a bender, doesn't pose much of a threat.'

I sense – lighting a cigarette – Anthony's curiosity; the questions he wants to ask: *Does size matter? Is sex better than a blow job? How does one give Good Head?* What, I wonder, would Anthony say about my own – sorry – sex life? The prospect of casual sex must seem, for him, as glamorous as it is unattainable. Or perhaps, in a quixotic sort of way, he'd see it for what it is: sordid, empty, trite.

Finally, he says: 'Well, I still think he should've married her.'

'I rather suspect that that's – eventually – what he does.'

32

In the evening I have supper with Sophie Fox, a notoriously hard-nosed literary agent – known, on both sides of the Atlantic, as The Bitch – who, I learn to my astonishment, is representing my mother in the States. Sophie's male secretary rang me up yesterday, and, having disdainfully explained who Ms Fox was, pencilled in a meeting at Quaglino's (possibly the ponciest restaurant in London) for Friday night.

By the time she arrives (forty-five minutes late) I am on my third champagne cocktail. For some reason – perhaps the hauteur of the bar staff, my surly desire to fuck the French cigarette girl, my exhaustless philistine lust – I am feeling terribly belligerent. Sophie, stylishly attired in a designer business suit, is in her early forties. While not exactly plump, she has an older woman's girth; a handsome, broad-boned, somehow wanton face, no doubt pampered with expensive cosmetics fraudulently promising perennial youth. For all her flirtatious banter with the maitre d' we are yet seated downstairs in the immense banqueting hall at a table next to the kitchen.

'So *I* said,' says Sophie, breezily approving our bottle of Sancerre, 'Look, let's quit screwing around here. Either you agree to my terms or I move my clients lock, stock and barrel to HarperCollins, and don't think that I won't. So this jerk-off says: You couldn't possibly break the contracts. So I'm like: Does a contract protect against writers' block? I don't *think* so. They signed the deal there and then.'

'Very impressive,' I say, acidly.

Sophie's clients, at least in this country, are far from prestigious. The male ones tend to write about sad single men, who, for all their droll self-deprecation and hilarious confessions of unrepentant self-abuse, are mysteriously unable to get laid; while the women write about, yes, sad single women, who are likewise erotically bereft, or, in their parlance, 'gagging for a shag'. That said, they are all depressingly successful, and one can only hope that their outrageous advances will enable them to find a compatible partner and to start writing about something else.

'Spineless. That's what you English are.'

'Better that than vulgar and brash.'

'Do you mind?' she says, when I light a cigarette.

'Do I mind what?'

'Not smoking.'

'Oh for Christ's sake.'

'Have you *read* the stats on passive smoking?'

'No. Have you read *Being and Time*?'

'That's Nietzsche, right?'

'No. Jean-Paul Sartre. He wrote the screenplay for *Independence Day*.'

'Don't bullshit me, Mat.'

'My name's Matthew, not "Mat".'

'Have I done something to offend you, Mat?'

'No.'

'Well then what's with the attitude?'

'Attitude?'

'I'm trying to help you, Mat. Remember that. I'm only doing this as a favour to your mother. You're not client material. So the least you can do is try and be polite.'

The waiter arrives with our starters. Scanning the balcony in the abject hope of catching a glimpse of the cigarette girl's panties, I see my mother descending the stairs with a swarthy Mediterranean pretty boy not much older than myself.

'So Tessy tells me you're writing a novel.'

'What?'

'I *said* —'

'Oh yes. No. I am,' I say, still watching Theresa and her beau over Sophie's shoulder as the maitre d' escorts them to an exclusive table at the far end of the hall.

'So you wanna tell me what's it about?'

I sheepishly outline the plot of my abandoned novel.

'Okay, Mat. I'm gonna be brutal here. I don't like it. In fact, I think it stinks. If you want my advice you should write a memoir.'

Stung by Sophie's pithy criticism, I ignore the remainder of my pan-fried fois gras and light a cigarette. 'And why would I want to do that?' I say, blowing smoke over her Caesar salad. Meanwhile, the maitre d' himself has brought a bottle of champagne to my mother's table.

'Because basically no one gives a shit about Jean-Paul Sartre,' says Sophie, bridling. 'Your job as a novelist, Mat, is to *entertain*, not to educate. People wanna read about stuff they've done. The shit that happens. And what could be more universal and sympathetic than the *angst* of growing up?'

'So you want me to write a book about masturbation, is that it?'

'Well, I don't think you should shy away from the subject, if that's what you mean.'

'What I *mean*,' I say angrily, maddened by the sight of my mother playing with her boyfriend's kinky hair, 'is that autobiography is a shitty art form. If I sell another memoir of some minor celebrity's battle with the bottle, some no-hoper's heroin addiction, some loser's obsession with fucking QPR – I don't know what I'm going to do!'

'You wouldn't be jealous now, would you, Mat?'

'Jealous?'

'Yeah, jealous. They're published and you're not. That's basically what it boils down to, isn't it?'

'Well, if I have to pander to the lowest common denominator, the crassest, most prurient sensibility, then I'd rather labour in obscurity.'

'Mat, will you listen to yourself. *Labour in obscurity*? It has a noble ring, I'll grant you that. But name me one famous writer that never made it in his lifetime. Shakespeare? Dante? Dickens? I don't *think* so.'

'Okay. John Kennedy Toole.'

'The name rings a bell.'

'He wrote *The Confederacy of Dunces* and killed himself out of despair of ever getting his manuscript published. Eventually, more than ten years later, his mother found a publisher willing to take it on and it was instantly acknowledged as a masterpiece and won the Pulizter Prize in 1981.'

'And he's your hero, is that it, Mat?'

'Well, no. But –'

'He sounds like a loser to me.'

'Oh fuck you. What would *you* know about literature?'

'You're kind of cute when you get angry, Mat. You know that?'

'*What*?'

'You ever had sex with an older woman?'

'Does my mother count?'

'Ha. You almost had me there.'

Unable to bear the spectacle of my mother with another man or the feel of Sophie's unshod foot caressing my shin, I announce: 'I'm going to the toilet.'

'Hurry on back, loverboy.'

As I storm through the frosted glass door into the lobby of the lavatory, I notice a pay phone to my left. On a whim, I fish through my jacket pocket for my mother's card, and dial the number of her mobile phone.

'What?' says Theresa imperiously.

'Put heem on,' I say, feebly imitating some Latino bad boy.

'Put who on? Who is this?'

'Please, signora, ees best I speak with heem.'

'Charles,' she says in the background, 'someone for you.'

'Hello,' says Charles in an impeccable English accent.

'You're a dead man,' I say truculently, trying to sound like Robert De Niro.

'What? Who is this?'

'I said you're fucking dead! There is a *dead man* on this line. You got that, you fucking cocksucking nancy-boy faggot!'

I'm tempted to smash the receiver to bits; however, being British, I simply hang up.

I'm about to enter the Gents when I hear my mother's voice behind me:

'Miff, darling, it's *you*. What are you doing here?'

'Mum?' I say turning round.

'*Sweetie*, you never call me mum,' sounding delighted. 'Come. Give Mummy a kiss.' Then, as I embrace her: 'Darling, whatever is the matter? You're trembling like a leaf.'

Bad Woman upset me, Mummy, I want to say. 'Nothing. I'm having dinner with Sophie Fox.'

'Oh *really*. I didn't see her.' Then, solicitously: 'Well isn't she being helpful?'

'No. She's not.'

'Darling, what on earth's she done?'

'She's crass, she's stupid and I hate her,' I say, enjoying my childish histrionics.

'Well she's *American*, what do you expect?'

'She's under the impression that you're *bosom buddies*.'

'Well, sometimes it *pays* to be charming.' Then, fondly caressing my hair: 'Now, I really must powder my nose.'

'Who's that man you're with?'

'Oh, Charles. He's . . . nobody. Just someone I met.'

'He's a bit young, isn't he?'

'Darling, you're not jealous are you?'

'No. Why should I be?'

'No reason,' she says leerily.

Standing at the urinal, disconcerted by the presence of the beliveried toilet attendant, I am unable to pee. Feeling somewhat akin to a thwarted toilet trader, I zip up my fly, wash my hands and leave an ostentatious tip.

As I rejoin Sophie, she says: 'Wasn't that your mother I just saw?'

'Yes. It was. She'll be out in a minute.'

Casually glancing at Theresa's table, I'm elated to see that it is empty. Charles has fled. As my mother approaches, she is intercepted by a waiter; having scanned the note, she disdainfully drops it on the salver as if rejecting a substandard vintage of Chateau Margaux.

'Tessy, *darling*,' says Sophie, standing up, arms outstretched.

'Sophie, *won*derful to see you,' says Theresa, kissing her on either cheek.

'What happened to your companion?' I ask as I seat her.

'Who, Charles?' she says, magicking a cigarette from her Gucci clutch. 'Oh, you know, business.' Then, after I light her fag: 'So, what have you two been talking about?'

'Well –' I begin.

'I was telling Mat that he should forget about fiction – at least for the time *being* – and write a memoir.'

'Whatever for? He hasn't *done* anything.'

'Sophie seems to think,' I interject, 'that everyone'll want to know how I used to toss off over the underwear section in the Freeman's catalogue.'

'Did you, darling? Really?' says Theresa, as if taken with the idea.

'You see, Mat,' says Sophie triumphantly. 'Even *Tessy's* intrigued.'

'His name's Matthew, not Mat.'

'That's what Mat said.'

'Well call him Matthew, then. Or Miff.'

'Miff? What kind of a name is Miff?'

'It's short for Matthew, *imbecile*.'

'Tessy, what's gotten into you?'

'And you can call *me*, Theresa.'

'*Okay*, Theresa. I thought we were friends.'

'So did I.'

'Look, *I'm* the one who's doing *you* a favour.'

'Is that what this is? I'd say you were trying to seduce him.'

'Don't be ridiculous.'

'Well then why didn't you arrange to meet him at your office?'

'I was busy.'

'But not too busy to take him to dinner on a Friday night? Look Sophie, everyone *knows* about your penchant for young men, why don't you just admit it.'

'And what about *your* penchant for young men?'

'What're you talking about? Miff's my son.'

'You could've fooled me. The way you act – *God* – it's as though you're his *lover*.'

'Come on, Miff. We're going.' Then, when I don't respond: 'I said,' peremptorily, '*we're going.*'

As a parting shot, Sophie says: 'I'm sure you'll both be very happy.'

'I'm sure,' says my mother tartly, 'we will.'

33

Saturday afternoon at Iseult's is especially abandoned. I absolutely cannot get enough. Yes, I am an animal. I have base desires. And whereas with Clare one feels that she enjoys her post-coital spliff rather more than the coitus itself – for Iseult sex is an all-consuming need. And, aside from her physical beauty, her taut willowy ballerina's bod, it is her relentless willingness that I find so unbearably erotic: For she'll never say no. Never have a headache. Never not be in the mood. Will surrender, endlessly, without surfeit, for as long as I can stand it. And when I cry, when it all becomes too much, Iseult is there to comfort me. She bathes me, dries me, washes and brushes my hair – and when I close my eyes I can almost believe myself her baby, exempt, if only for an afternoon, from grown-up fears and responsibilities. However, I can't shake the feeling that there is something inexpressibly sinister behind her infant fetish. Of course, I cannot ask her, but I rather wonder whether she uses a contraceptive of some sort – or, rather, if she isn't deliberately attempting to conceive a *bona fide* Naughty Boy of her own. Perhaps, like many another *femme fatale*, she simply wants me to do away with her husband. *Miff*, she'll say, *if my husband found out about us he'd kill you. He'd kill us both. Do you want that, Miff? Is that what you want?* Hell no. Conveniently, she'll already have thought up a foolproof plan. Then, when the dastardly deed is done she'll betray me and I'll take the fall for her husband's death. *You know the sad thing is, Jimmy,* I'll tell the warden as he leads me to the electric chair, *I'm still in love with her.* Cut to the warden, who has been narrating the story to a stranger in a bar: *Yup*, he'll say, *she sure was one sick twist.* Cut to the stranger: *Well I'll be darned.*

Halfway through my lesson (M is for Mummy: a radiant self-portrait in pastel), Iseult excuses herself ('Mummy go peepee') and goes to the loo. Idly gazing at the plan-chest, I notice that the bottom drawer (the one from which Iseult removed her alphabet pictures) is partially open. At first it appears empty; however, nestled at the back I find an unmounted charcoal sketch somewhat reminiscent of Käthe Kollwitz: Iseult squats in the corner of a wall, a – her? – baby is fiercely enfolded in her arms; both are naked: and from the look of vivid terror on her face one can only infer that the infant's – and possibly her own – life is in danger; even the sky – stormy, infuriate – seems freighted with calamity. I'm so engrossed I scarcely register the toilet flush, the bathroom door open, the sound of Iseult's rapid approach. 'Naughty Boy! Put that back!' 'What?' I reply innocently. Iseult's tasselled riding crop comes crashing down on my padded backside. 'Jesus!' Again the smarting, somehow pleasurable, pain. 'I'm sorry.' So intolerable is my capacity to speak, that Iseult decides to thrash me good and proper. 'Never . . . play . . . with Mummy's . . . things,' she berates, between punitive lashes. Feeling somewhat resentfully that she has gone too far, I resolve on an infantile act of rebellion – and, *sans* preamble, piss my pants. But far from making my indignation felt, my nappy-wetting provokes in Iseult pleasant surprise ('Oh, Naughty Boy!'), and as my urine trickles across the bare floorboards she dashes to the kitchen, and, returning with a dishcloth, delightedly proceeds to mop it all up.

34

'True love,' I tell Anthony, 'always ends in tragedy.'

'But *why*?' he says, almost angrily. He has just finished reading *Romeo and Juliet* and is outraged by its — as he sees it — gratuitously tragic denouement.

'Because if they absconded to Scunthorpe and had a couple of kids it wouldn't be love.'

'Why wouldn't it?'

'Because true *lovers* don't go shopping at Safeway. They don't *potter* around Do-It-All on a Sunday afternoon.'

'What are you talking about?'

'Look, the reason why Cupid is generally depicted wearing a blindfold is because his *darts* are as much a bane as a benison.'

'Bane? Benison?' says Anthony despairingly.

'A bane is a curse,' I intone piously, 'and a benison is a blessing.'

'Well then why not *say* a curse and a blessing?'

'Okay, I confess, I said it deliberately to flummox you. In fact, the reason why Shakespeare employs such high-flown language isn't, as scholars have speculated, for its poetic effect, but because you wouldn't feel stupid if he hadn't!'

Anthony looks furious. 'But *why*,' he whines, 'do Romeo and Juliet have to die?'

'Because it'd be aesthetically unsatisfactory if they didn't. Because Romeo, if he'd have arrived later and found Juliet alive, wouldn't have been able to utter the immortal lines: "Here, here will I remain/ With worms that are thy chambermaids. O, here/ Will I set up my everlasting rest,/ And shake the yoke of inauspicious stars/ From this world-wearied flesh." No, he'd have had to've said: "Juliet, thank fuck I found you. Come, let's hie us to Skegness."'

Anthony, in spite of himself, laughs. Then, remembering his righteous indignation: 'So you're saying that Shakespeare killed them off for the sake of a good story?'

'Well, to be fair, his play was based on a poem by Arthur Brooke – but yes! Yes yes yes! In fact, I'll go you one further and say that *true* love – terrible, godawful, soul-tormenting love – ends with thanatos!'

'Thanatos?'

'Death! Orpheus and Eurydice, Tristan and Isolde, Heathcliff and Catherine – I don't know – Vronsky and Anna Karenina!'

'It's sad,' says Anthony.

'It's a goddamned tragedy!'

Then, shyly: 'Have you ever been in love?'

'Once,' I say wistfully, 'I thought I was.'

'What happened?'

'Nothing. I was five years old. It was a girl I sat next to in primary school.'

'Oh,' he says, a tad disappointed. Then, timorously: 'I'm in love.'

'Really? Who with?'

'Oh,' airily, 'you wouldn't know her.' Then, beginning to blush: 'Miss Collins. My English teacher.'

Anthony, Anthony. 'And does Miss Collins love you?'

'She . . . likes me. I think.'

'And, what, you think that if Miss Collins fell in love with you you'd be happy?'

'Well, yes.'

'For ever and ever?'

'For ever and ever,' he declares. 'Yes.'

'Okay, let's say for the sake of argument that she does.'

'What?'

'Love you.'

'Oh, okay.'

'How d'you feel?'

'Well, happy. I'm in love. Isn't that how you're meant to feel?'

'Sure. But let's not forget about the worry.'

'Worry?'

'I mean, heaven forfend, when you're not with her she could be killed, raped, hideously maimed.'

'But –'

'And then there's the jealousy.'

'Jealousy?'

'Absolutely. Who's she with now? Is she having an affair? Why was she flirting with your best friend? Who the fuck called last night at 3 am, and why did he hang up when you answered?'

'But . . . we're in love. She wouldn't want to be with anyone else.'

'Oh, that's what you'd tell yourself. In the beginning. But pretty soon you'd be lying awake at night thinking about your wife being fucked by other men – friends, colleagues, acquaintances – butchers, bakers, candlestick-makers – remember, paranoia's just as plausible as truth.'

'But why would I be paranoid?'

'Because you'd feel guilty. Why does she love me? What've I done to deserve her? Why should I feel happy when everyone else feels like shit?'

'And how would you know?' says Anthony, obviously outraged. 'You've never been in love.'

'Well, no. But I have it on good authority.'

'*Whose?*'

'Oh, you know – Updike, Mailer, Roth.'

'And they're writers I suppose?'

'American writers, yes.'

'And what if they're wrong?'

'Then we'll all live happily ever after.'

35

After work, Judy, Steve, Victoria, Clare, Kay and myself head off to the Prototype Gallery on Marylebone High Street for the opening night of Phil's 'anti-show': THERE IS NO GOD. The vestibule is dominated by William McWilliam's 'Black Death' – a massive canvas painted, or rather spattered, uniformly black. 'All *right*,' says Steve approvingly. Victoria, like a startled, heartrendingly undernourished fawn, remains transfixed by the painting while the rest of us bustle into the main gallery. Scanning the crowd I see that most of the full-timers – who've been here since they left The Book Shop at half past six – are already conspicuously pissed. Predictably, they are massed around the trestle tables at the far end of the gallery that serve as a makeshift bar. 'Oi, Judy!' shrieks Patricia as we enter. 'Heard you fucked a *hob*goblin' – cruelly referring to her fling with the dwarf – 'atta girl!' 'Did someone call me?' asks Judy, blessedly oblivious. 'It were that fat cow over there,' says Clare, coming to her defence.

On my way to the bar I bump into Phil. He is wearing a superbly tight white T-shirt with a fetching breast pocket; canvas Vans; blue jeans.

'Philippe! Bonsoir.'

'Bonsoiree, ma cherry,' he says gaily, kissing me on either cheek.

'Phil,' I say, tremendously touched, 'people will say we're in love.'

'But we are in love.' Then, having downed the remainder of his plastic beaker of wine: 'Je tame.'

'So what's the deal with the drinks?'

'Oh, help yourself. I'm telling you, I'm *ab*solutely trunche-oned. I get so *nervous* – I've been drinking all day.' Then: 'Where's Iseult?'

'She couldn't come.'

'But *why*? She said she would.'

'I'm not sure.'

'Oh.' Phil seems genuinely hurt. 'D'you think she's got a boyfriend?'

Or a husband? Or a son? Suddenly feeling equally upset, I

say: 'No.' Then: 'Surely not.' Then, to cheer him up: 'Super outfit.'

'*Really*? D'you like it?'

'Phil, I *love it*.'

'I love you, too,' he says.

At the bar I help myself to a cupful of KostKutter Red – possibly the cheapest nastiest wine known to man.

'God, Howard, what're you *like*?' says Patricia.

'Klingon,' says Howard, who bears a disconcerting resemblance to Tintin. '*Kling*on. Kling*on*. *Klingon*.'

Nodding at me, Patricia says: 'Hey Howard, Miff had sex with your *wife*.'

'Klingon,' says Howard.

'What's up with him?'

'God, Howard's really *fucked*. He did about a hundred magic mushrooms in the staffroom – made me want to *chuck*.' Then, staring frankly at my crotch: 'Hey, Butch.'

Oh fuck. 'What?'

Grabbing hold of my belt – presumably for support – she stands on tiptoe and whispers in my ear: 'Nice *packet*.'

Jesus! 'Um. Thanks.'

After downing my wine, I pour myself two more cups of red and join Steve. Since I found out he's fucking Clare I've felt an odd, almost fraternal, bond between us – a bizarre species of brotherly love. He is appraising an installation by Matte Black: an enormous toy cow lies on its back with its legs in the air; the word *McDeath* has been branded – or rather scrawled in Magic Marker – on its chest.

'So, Steve,' I say, 'what d'you see in this?'

'Man, it's like nothing I've ever seen. It's hard to describe. But I'll tell you this – I'll never fucking *never* eat meat again.'

'If you ask me, it's a load of old wank.'

'Christ, Miff. How can you *say* that? Just look at it.'

'I am.'

'Can't you see the beauty – the fucking *poetry* – of the idea? It's like an extraordinarily moral – I don't know – metaconceptual piece of propaganda.'

'Metaconceptual my arse. Christ, it's about as subtle as tattooing DON'T EAT MEAT on your fucking forehead. Propaganda, yes. Art, no. And as for "Black Death" –'

'Masterpiece.'

'Of pretension, maybe. But, Christ – *I* could've painted it. I could've painted it with the paint brush up my *arse*.'

'But that's the whole point. It's the *concept* that's important – not the execution.'

'Oh that's bollocks. Everyone thinks they've got a good idea for a novel – only for most of them it's all they can do to spell their own fucking name, much less parse a sentence. You ever heard of the indefinite article, Steve? Would you recognise a split infinitive?'

'Ah! There's no talking to you,' he says, and stalks off towards the bar.

On an impulse, I return to the vestibule, where I find Victoria still spellbound by 'Black Death'. After offering her a cup of wine, which she ignores – indeed, stares straight ahead of her the whole time – she finally says:

'Death . . . is black.'

'Verily,' I say.

'"Darkling I listen; and for many a time/ I have been half

in love with easeful Death,/ Call'd him soft names in many a mused rhyme,/ To take into the air my quiet breath" – '

'"Now more than ever seems it rich to die,/ To cease upon the midnight with no pain,/ While thou art pouring forth thy soul abroad/ In such an ecstasy!/ Still wouldst thou sing, and I have ears in vain –/ To thy high requiem become a sod."

'I sometimes think . . . about death. Do you think suicides go to heaven? In the *Inferno* they're turned to trees and attacked by Harpies.'

'Victoria, what's wrong?'

Eventually, in the uninflected tones of someone in a state of hypnosis – or, simply, shock – she says:

'I had a meeting today at Poetaster Press. They said they didn't like my poetry but they liked my image. They said anorexia was in. They said that after the success of Elizabeth Wurtzel they wanted to issue a collection called *Prozac Fuck-Up* – and that if I couldn't write poems about anorexia and Prozac they'd find someone else who could. But they'd still pay me for appearing naked on the front cover. And that as long as I changed my name to Barbara San Diego, even if someone else wrote the poems I could still pretend that they were mine.'

'Well fuck them. I never thought Poetaster were worthy of you anyway. You should submit your work to Chatto & Windus instead.'

'I already did.'

'Well then, Faber & Faber.'

'Yeah,' says Clare, standing behind me in the doorway. 'Do you think Chatterton regrets committing suicide?'

'I'm sure he does.' Then, tactlessly: 'Just think of all the . . . *shagging* he missed out on.'

'*Miff*,' says Clare. Then, as Victoria starts to cry: '*Ah*, yer poor thing. Come 'ere.' And, as she enfolds her brittle, pathetically birdlike body in her arms, with an impatient nod of the head, motions for me to leave.

Back in the gallery, having somehow consumed both cups of red, I refuel at the bar (taking care to avoid Patricia) and wander over to where Judy and Kay are discussing Philippe Aujourd'hui's 'Mad About the Rabbit' – basically, an enlarged photocopy of Bugs Bunny wearing a crudely limned leather bondage cap.

'Why's he wearing that hat?' asks Kay.

'It does look odd,' says Judy unsteadily. 'I think it's something to do with S&M.'

'What's S&M?'

'Superman,' I say. 'Yes, Superman used to wear that cap.'

'He did?'

'Well, perhaps not in the films. But in the comics he did.'

'Oh, I thought . . .' with unspeakable timidity: 'Didn't Clark Kent wear a trilby?'

'To the office, sure. But when he went clubbing –'

'Clark Kent went "clubbing"?'

'Actually, he was never that into it. But as for Lois – well, she sure was *one* crazy hepcat.'

Such is Kay's consternation, I almost admit to having made the whole thing up. Meanwhile, Judy has been studying Phil's companion piece 'Funny Bunny' – in which Bugs's customary carrot has been transformed into a Bob Marley-size spliff. 'I think I prefer "Mad About the Rabbit".'

'That's a big cigarette,' says Kay.

'Shall you tell her or shall I?'

'It's called a king-size cigarette,' I say.

'Oh.'

Then, wanting desperately to hug her: 'Kay . . .'

'Yes, Miff.'

Come live with mee, and be my love. 'You haven't got a drink.'

'No.' Then: 'Have they got any cider?'

'I'm afraid not. Only wine.'

'Bloody good stuff,' says Judy, already floozled. Then, staring at my cigarette: 'Ooh, give us a ciggie, Miff.'

I offer her the pack. Before taking one out she looks to her right and left like a schoolgirl checking for teachers before sparking up in her lunch break. Predictably, like many another social smoker, Judy doesn't inhale; after holding the smoke in her mouth for a moment, she exhales like a bellows, as if her very innards are ablaze.

Feeling mischievous, I tell her: 'You know, I get nightmares about your arse?'

'I beg your pardon?'

'I said: I think this show's a *farce.*'

'*Oh*' – looking mightily relieved – 'I thought you said . . .'

'What?'

Exhaling another messy zeppelin of smoke. 'Never mind.'

In the toilets I find Howard staring in psychotic wonderment at his reflection in the mirror. 'The horror . . .' he whispers, touching his fingertips to the glass. 'The *horror.*' While waiting for a vacant cubicle, I hear the torrential spatter of someone puking up. After a moment's astonished silence, a great chorus of cheers issues from the other stalls. 'Way to go!' shouts someone. 'Fuck, yeah,' cries another. 'The chunder express has *arrived*,' says a third, seemingly in the same cubicle – whence Charlie and Ed (two of the full-timers) presently emerge. Both of them – in order, I suppose, to obviate any slurs on their sexuality – sniff loudly and make a pantomime of preening their noses in the mirror. 'Oi, Howard,' says Ed, 'your wife got abducted by *aliens*.' 'Yeah,' says Charlie, 'she's carrying an alien up her *arse*.' Entering their vacated cubicle, I find Patricia chopping up monster lines of whizz with her Barclaycard.

'Hey, Butch,' she says.

Oh fuck, not again. 'Peepee, what a pleasant surprise.'

She is sitting on top of the toilet lid. Her legs are spread to such a degree that, beneath her short black skirt, I can clearly see the cottony pink carapace of her panties. Using a rolled-up ten-pound note, she hunches over her vanity mirror and does a line. 'You want some?'

'Er, no – thanks.'

'God, Miff, you're such a *mummy's* boy.'

All right, that does it. 'Sure, I'll do a line,' I say, instantly regretting my bravado. Feigning nonchalance, I take the ten-pound note and gingerly hover up one of the whitish lines of powder. Expecting – I don't know – a potent influx of euphoria I'm disappointed to find that the most immediate effect is a disagreeable bitterness at the back of my mouth.

'There, Butch, that wasn't so bad now, was it?'

'No,' I say, trying not to sneeze.

'So I hear you're fucking Clare.'

'Who told you that?'

'Someone.' Then: 'You should know she's *fucked* almost everyone at work – male *and* female.'

'Really.'

'Yeah. *Really.*' Then: 'So why is it –' noisily snorting another line – 'you've never tried to fuck me?'

'I've been busy,' I say, suddenly feeling tremendously – somehow sexually – energetic.

I find myself staring fixedly at her panties; seeing this, Patricia grabs my hand and thrusts it between her legs. Needing no more prompting, I fairly hoist her to her feet and lunge at her mouth. We kiss clumsily, frenetically, our teeth clitting, Patricia drawing blood. I have by now burrowed my hand beneath her panties and roughly plugged two fingers in her cunt. Patricia, who has clamped both hands around my butt, suddenly – breathlessly – says: 'Wait.' Locking the door, she pulls her panties down around her ankles, and, clasping hold of either side of the cistern, bends over. Lifting up her skirt, I'm struck by a high muttony stink, and, pulling out my prick, discover that I'm – at best – only barely tumescent. 'Come on, Butch, what the fuck are you waiting for?'

Panicking, I slot three fingers inside her and, with my right hand, attempt to wank myself erect. 'Enough with the fingers already,' says Patricia, '*I want your meat.*' 'Oh, fuck,' groans the fellow next door – possibly Phil – followed by yet another cataract of puke. *What the fuck am I doing?* I think, suddenly struck by the utter abjectivity of where I am and what I'm doing – or, rather, attempting to do. Just then there is a knock at the door. 'P., open up, it's Ed.' (Ed is one of Patricia's numerous beaux.) 'Shit,' she says, hiking up her panties. As I hastily rearrange myself, I make a loud snorting noise – and, opening the door, ostentatiously rub my nostrils. 'Hey, Ed,' I say. Then, confidentially: 'Good shit.'

Back in the gallery I down several cups of wine in order to quell my twitchy hyperactivity. Searching the crowd I spot Clare betranced by an installation entitled 'Human Excrement' – however, as I approach, I see that what lurks behind the glass isn't *homo sapiens* faeces but a common-or-garden cowpat.

'How's Victoria?' I ask.

'Judy's lookin' after 'er. They left in a cab ten minutes ago.'

'So she'll be okay?'

'I 'ope so. I think what Poetaster did is bang out of order, though. In fact, it's fockin' tragic.'

'Absolutely.' Then, apropos Roddy Rubens's 'Human Excrement': 'So what d'you think?'

'Ah, it's great. It's like me project on waste. I think 'e's tryin' to expose the animal side of 'uman nature – the same as me.'

'But it's a fucking cowpat,' I protest.

'Exactly. 'E's juxtaposin' animal an' 'uman shit – as if to say: What's the difference?'

'Well, a cowpat's bigger for one thing.'

'Miff, that's not the point.'

'Well what is the point?' I say aggressively.

'The point,' says a begoateed, black-clad stranger with round tinted-orange specs, 'is that it's *all* shit. The democracy of excrement.'

'Pro-fucking-found.'

'*Miff*,' says Clare. Then: 'I'm sorry. We 'aven't been introduced yet. I'm Clare.'

'Bill McWilliam,' he says.

'An' this is Miff.'

'Miff. Hi.' Then: 'I sense you're somewhat sceptical.'

'Of what?'

'Well, of our work.'

'It's not so much scepticism – it's far more damning than that – I think it's *devoid* of artistic merit.'

'Don't mind Miff,' says Clare apologetically, '''e's a cultural Tory.'

'I am not.'

''E thinks art started an' ended with what's'isname? – da Vinci.'

'Oh that's bullshit. Some of my favourite artists are twentieth century.'

'Such as?' asks Bill.

'Dix, Schiele, Schad.'

'Old hat.'

'And who the fuck are *your* favourite painters then?'

'I don't have any.'

'Me neither,' says Clare.

'So you've never been influenced by anyone?'

'Well, in terms of sacrifice and bravery, I suppose I've been *inspired* by Stolid Grunge. But then again – who hasn't?'

(Stolid catapulted himself to overnight celebrity by paying a couple of penurious medics to remove his right kidney. In a nice irony, the surgeon who'd originally been approached to perform the procedure was called in to repair the damage after Stolid suffered renal failure in the aftermath of his botched operation. After three weeks of dialysis, Stolid was released from hospital. His resultant installation, 'Loneliness' –

his ravaged right kidney in a fishtank of formaldehyde –
received rapturous acclaim and was purchased for £100,000
by Charles Saatchi.)

'*I* haven't. If you ask me, Stolid *Grunge* is a fucking
arsehole.'

'*Miff*,' says Clare, 'you're talkin' 'bout Bill's 'ero.'

'I'm sorry, but the man's a charlatan. In fact, you're *both*
charlatans.'

'Look, just because you've failed to make the paradigm
shift between figurative and *conceptual* art, doesn't mean –'

'You think you're so radical,' I thunder, 'when you've no
knowledge of the tradition you're *supposedly* rebelling
against.'

'– that Clare's and my work – or, for that matter,
conceptual art in general – is worthless. If you were an *artist*
you'd appreciate –'

'Name a Fauvist. Name an Abstract Expressionist. Name a
Futurist. You can't, can you?'

'Matisse. Grosz. And . . .'

'Of course, it's not your fault. Goldsmith's and the like are
just too damn *trendy* to teach anything as hopelessly old-
fashioned as chiaroscuro or perspective – let alone history of
art. Tell me, Bill. If I gave you a bowl of fruit could you even
sketch it? Could you, Clare?'

'That's not the point.'

'Severini,' says Bill. 'And, as it happens, yes I could.'

'You know what's sad, Bill? In twenty years' time people
are going to look back at the nineties and wonder what the
fuck you were all doing. And whilst your *shit*'ll doubtless win

you a grotesque circus of celebrity, the work of *real* artists'll be forgotten!'

Bill can only shake his head in weary contempt. Spying Kay, who has wandered over to see what the ruckus is about (hoping, no doubt, to defuse the situation), I say: 'Come on, Kay, we're going.'

'We are?' she says.

'Yes' — as if our leaving together will somehow vindicate my thesis — '*we are.*'

36

The following morning I find myself in Kay's bed, alongside a diminutive menagerie of cuddly toys. 'Good morning, my love,' she says, her head on my chest, her small girl's tits tickling my flank. *Please, God. No*, I think, before instantly recalling our Night of Passion. Spurred on by the speed, I made a pass at her in the back of the cab. Kay, while limply passive, none the less swooned and sighed and more than once cried, 'Oh Miff!' Back at her place, she insisted on disrobing in the dark. '*Miff*,' she whispered, once we were in bed. 'Yes, Kay?' 'Before we . . . *start*, I want you to know . . .' 'What, Kay? What?' 'I mean, it's only *fair* that you should know . . .' 'I don't care! Anything! What?' 'That, well . . . I'm married.' *Married!* 'But, Kay . . .' *Surely, you're a virgin.* 'But we're getting a divorce,' she hastily assured me. 'We've been separated for more than six months.' Then, when I didn't answer: 'If you want, I could . . . *you* know . . .

suck your willy. I don't *mind*.' Such, alas, was my drug-inspired stamina, that, after half an hour of indifferent, albeit (on my part) energetic, fucking (during which Kay, despite the odd defenceless whimper, showed no signs of coming – or, for that matter, enjoyment – whatsoever) I had recourse to faking my orgasm.

'Miff,' she says, suddenly ominously still (she has been raptly caressing my chest).

'Yes?'

'Say it's true.'

'What is?'

'That you love me. That you've always loved me. That you loved me from the minute that we met.'

'Christ, Kay.'

'Yes, I feel it too. It's always been you.'

'What has?'

'Oh, darling, let's not pretend any more. Let people speak. Shout it in the streets, proclaim it from the rooftops – tell the whole wide world: *We're* in *love!*'

'Kay, where're you getting this? Are you quoting from a film?'

'Darling, can't you see it yet? It's the film of our life.'

'What life? We don't have a life. Kay, I don't love you.'

'There you go again, darling – denying our love.'

'Kay, look at me,' I say sitting up – and only then do I see that she is crying. 'Christ, Kay. I'm sorry. Okay. I'm sorry about last night. I really, really . . .' but even as I utter them my words seem inapt, insulting, derisory.

'You'd love me if I was a "bitch".'

'Kay, I love you as a friend because you're *not* a bitch.'

'You love Iseult. You love Clare.'

Christ, does everybody know? 'No. I don't. I don't "love" anyone. Perhaps that's my problem.'

'My husband, when he left me, he said I was too nice. He said he couldn't stand my "niceness". He said I should get angry, throw plates – have affairs.'

Looking at her pale prepubescent breasts, it's all I can do not to cry. *If only*, I think, *I could love Kay.* 'Well he sounds like an arse,' trying to console her. 'You're too good for him.'

'But that's just it,' wails Kay: 'I'm too good. I'm too nice. *Oh*, I'm going to be a spinster, I just know it.'

'You won't,' I tell her. Then, helplessly: 'You just won't.'

37

Preparing to leave, patting down my pockets in the hallway, I hear a familiar voice behind me. Turning around, I see Liz – my ex-girlfriend – looking sexily dishevelled in a crumpled nightshirt.

'Liz . . . what're you doing here?'

'I live here. What are *you* doing here?'

'Nothing.'

'You didn't . . .'

'No.'

'You slept with my sister, didn't you?'

'Yes. No. I don't know.' Then: 'Yes.'

'Oh my God, I think I'm going to be sick.' Then, half-sitting on the back of the sofa: 'I can't *believe* you. No wait, maybe I can.'

'It's not what you think, Liz.'

'Hang on. Let me get this straight. We're talking about *Kay*' – contemptuously – 'my frumpy older sister?'

'Ssh. She'll hear you.'

'She's running a *bath*, she won't hear anything.' Then: 'Really, Miff, I thought you had more taste. I mean, Kay's an absolute Beryl if I say it myself, and I'm her sister.'

'I never did like you, Liz.'

'Oh, *now* I'm hurt.'

'She's worth a thousand of you.'

'Pah*lease*.' Then, as I turn to leave: 'No wait! Just answer me this.'

'What?' I say, my hand on the door.

Ripping open her nightshirt, she says: 'Who would you rather *boff* – her or me?'

38

On Wednesday, just before we sally forth on to the shop floor, Cynthia convenes a staff meeting. As usual she is clad in her butch business suit – I for one have never seen her wear anything else. Rumour has it that, like some crackpot scientist who simply can't be doing with such day-to-day decisions, she only has one outfit. Queasily, I imagine her undressing before bed: as soon as her skirt hits the floor it scuttles from the room like a terrified alien and throws itself into the maw of her washing machine; likewise, her jacket sets off at a rapid clip for the dry cleaner's. Cynthia shows no mercy: the rugby-tackled jacket is locked away in a dank closet; the skirt, after a severe ticking off, imprisoned in a chest of drawers.

'Now, as you all know,' says Cynthia, 'over the past few weeks there've been an unacceptable number of till *discrepancies*. After detailed *scrutiny* of the journal rolls, I've come to the conclusion that –' suddenly turning on Steve – '*Gum.*'

'Wha?'

'Gum. You're chewing gum. No chewing.'

'But –'

'No buts. Spit it out, boy.'

After noisily swallowing, Steve says: 'What gum?' And, to prove his innocence, opens his mouth and sticks out his tongue.

'Put that *away*. Really! Now, where was I? Oh yes. After detailed *scrutiny* of the journal rolls I've come to the conclusion that someone's been stealing. Yes, I said *stealing*. We have a *miscreant* in our midst. Now, I'm not necessarily saying that it's any of you – it could be one of the full-timers or someone on the other shift. *However* –' casting her basilisk eye over each of us, who, like guilty felons in a line-up, stare fixedly at the floor – 'we can't afford to rule anyone out – except, of course, myself.'

Attempting to lighten the atmosphere, I say: 'But Cynthia, surely, you have my word as a *gentleman* . . .'

Cynthia looks at me darkly; scribbles a note on her clipboard. 'You think this is a joke, do you, Miff? Well let me tell you – this is *serious*. Thou shalt not steal. And I'm going to personally see to it that the *perpetrator* is punished – and punished *severely*.'

'Pain force endure,' says Phil sententiously.

''Ow much is missin'?' asks Clare.

'By my calculations, over the past four weeks, four pounds and seventy-three pence. Now, rather than going to the police, head office thought it best to conduct an internal *inquiry*. Our chief of security – James Hawthornedon-Smythe – will be heading up the investigation. He and Rez will interview each of you tonight. And I would advise anyone with any information *pertaining* to this case to speak up now – or suffer the consequences. And, let me assure you, the consequences will be *grave*.'

After Cynthia leaves, Kay says: 'Well I didn't do it.'

'None of us did,' says Clare.

'How can you be so sure,' says Steve suspiciously. 'Why did Kay deny it?'

'Because I *didn't*.'

'Methinks thou dost protest too much.'

'Well I think it's out*rageous*,' says Judy. 'All this fuss over forty-nine pee.'

'Obviously, this was no ordinary caper,' says Steve. 'This was the work of a criminal mastermind.'

'D'you think if I confess,' says Phil hopefully, 'they'll make me wear *hand*cuffs?'

'I think they'll lock you in a cell,' I tell him, 'with sex-starved perverts.'

'Ooh, *don't*.'

'I can't believe they're puttin' that tosser in charge,' says Clare. 'The man thinks 'e's 007.'

And indeed James Hawthornedon-Smythe – once, I'll wager, Jim Smith – does like to pretend he's a secret agent. The first time I met him he sidled up to me while I was working on the till, flashed his badge and said: 'Smythe – James Hawthornedon-Smythe. At your service.' Another time, leafing through *Fuck With Me Not*, he remarked: 'Of course, I know Nutter.' When I asked him whether he'd ever been in the SAS, he suavely raised one eyebrow and said: ''Fraid I can't tell you, old man. Need-to-know basis, and all that.' However, he did intimate that he'd once worked for Her Majesty's Secret Service – more than that, though, he couldn't say. 'Of course I *could* tell you,' he went on to add. 'But then I'd have to kill you. And we don't want that, now, do we?' And then James is terribly fond of what he refers to as his gadgets. 'I wouldn't touch that, if I were you,' he once told Steve, who'd made the mistake of picking up his pen. 'Or what?' he rejoined, defiantly depressing the button. 'World War III?' James's pen, thus activated, emitted a high-pitched whine, prompting staff and customers alike to scrabble for cover while Steve stayed rooted to the spot; finally, to the sound of abject flatulence, it spurted ink all over the floor. But if James contrives to sound like Roger Moore he certainly doesn't share his stature: in his early forties he is a paunchy five feet four with thinning greyish-brown hair combed horizontally over his pate. And whereas most of the store detectives dress like hoods, James affects a martial mufti – navy brass-buttoned blazers, natty open-necked shirts, cravats, khaki chinos, and, unvaryingly, black elbow-greased Oxfords.

39

At half past nine, I am the last member of staff to be interviewed. On my way to Cynthia's office I pass Victoria, who, looking dangerously, cadaverously pale, is evidently too traumatised to speak. The first thing I notice upon entering the office is that the furniture has been rearranged: Cynthia's desk has been shifted to the centre of the room, and – presumably to create enough space to pace back and forth behind the interviewee – her filing cabinets have been removed.

'Take a seat,' says James genially, indicating the chair opposite his. Then, perceiving my apprehension: 'Re*lax*. We're just going to ask you a couple of questions, that's all.'

'Yeah man. Relax yo *mind*,' says Rez, who, standing just inside the door with his arms folded, has for some reason decided to affect a thick West Indian accent.

'So . . . shall we begin?'

'Go ahead,' I say.

On the table in front of me there is a tape recorder – however, rather than using it to record our conversation, James simply presses play. After a second or so I hear a monotonous dripping noise: *plink . . . plink . . . plink*. If my first impulse is to laugh, I'm none the less unnerved by this peculiarly sinister soundtrack. Inevitably, it seems, the main light is switched off and an angle-poise lamp trained bedazzlingly in my face. Rez, who ordinarily doesn't smoke, lights a cigarette and stands behind me, leaning both hands against the back of my chair. After blowing a concentrated plume of smoke in my face, he says:

'We know jew did it, mon.'

'Did what?'

'We know jew da teef.'

'Look here, old man,' says James in a positively bedside manner. 'Why not make it easy on yourself?'

'How?'

'Well, by telling the truth.'

'I didn't do it.'

'Now dat's jes not de troof,' says Rez, who has set to pacing behind me.

'I'm telling you the truth, I didn't take it.'

'Take what?' says James.

'The money.'

'And what money might that be?'

'The money that's gone missing.'

'So you're telling me there's money gone missing, are you?'

'No – *you're* telling *me*.'

'I don't believe I told you that. Perhaps I'm mistaken. Rez, did I or did I not tell young Matthew here money had gone missing?'

'No, mon.'

'So what can you tell us about this –' pausing theatrically – '"missing money"?'

'Nothing.'

'But you told us it was missing.'

'Yes, but . . .' insanely exasperated. 'Look, enough with this Tom and Jerry shit. I didn't take it, *okay?*'

'Take what?'

'Oh you fucking *know* what. Christ! Just lay down the whip, maybe I'll respect you more.'

Rez leaves off from pacing to slam his fist down on the table, and says: 'Why jew wanna be fuckin wid us?'

'I'm not fucking with you – I'm telling you the truth!'

'Jew's a *liar*, mon!'

As Rez advances the coal of his cigarette towards my right eye, the tape comes to a stop.

'Damn,' says James, 'I'll have to rewind it. Rez, turn the lights on.'

And, within seconds, sanity is restored: the light is turned on, the angle-poise switched off; Rez gratefully extinguishes his cigarette.

'So have you seen *Fargo* yet?' says Rez as the tape rewinds, reverting to his normal accent.

'Um . . . yeah,' is all I can say.

'Wicked film.'

'Yes, I rather enjoyed it,' says James amiably. 'Of course, I found the police procedure somewhat suspect – given, ahem, my training.'

'D'you mind if I smoke?' I ask timidly.

'Be my guest,' says James – even, as with trembling hands I place the cigarette in my mouth, he reaches across the table to light it.

'Smoking,' says Rez shaking his head. 'Bad habit.'

'Oh, I don't know,' says James. 'You can't beat a good pipe.'

'Pipe smoking's different – you don't inhale. But cigarettes – they're killers.'

Finally, to my terror, the tape is rewound. Off goes the light, on comes the angle-poise . . . *plink plink plink.*

'Gimme dat,' says Rez, snatching the cigarette I've been drawing on as if for dear life.

'Now, where were we,' says James. 'Oh yes. You were going to tell me where you hid the "missing money". Please, go ahead.'

Twenty minutes later, I am officially fired by Cynthia. For, while I stood up under questioning, when I emptied my pockets it transpired that I had on my person precisely four pounds and seventy-three pence. When I objected that if indeed I was the thief I wouldn't be so foolish as to keep the stolen money on me at work – which, moreover, was pilfered piecemeal over a number of weeks – James responded by saying that that's exactly what the thief *would* say, and that, as a sometime intelligence agent, if he was the thief that's exactly what he'd do. And try as I might to refute the charges, whatever I said seemed only to consolidate my guilt, until finally even *I* was unsure of my own innocence.

The Book Shop, I'm informed by Cynthia, believes in clemency. As long as I return the money they won't press charges with the police. However, she reminds me that stealing is still a sin – and, as such, will be punished by Him. 'I hope you realise,' she says with sacerdotal solemnity, 'the *enormity* of what you've done. If you don't, there's no hope for you. I shall *pray* for your soul.' 'But Cynthia –' I try to protest. 'So go down,' sternly interrupting me, 'and sin no more.'

40

On Sunday I have lunch with my father. As I walk up the drive to his semi-detached Edwardian house, I guiltily reflect that I haven't visited since I moved out back in January – and even though we've spoken on the phone a couple of times, I don't doubt that if it wasn't for his birthday (he is forty-eight today) I wouldn't be here. When he answers the door – dressed, pathetically, in baggy beige cords, a diamond-cut cardigan, an open-neck shirt – I make to embrace him; however, despite the fact that I suspect he mourns the passing of our physical intimacy just as much as me, we simply, awkwardly shake hands.

'Matthew. Good to see you,' he says trying to sound hearty.

'Happy birthday, Dad.'

'Thanks.' Then, still dithering on the doorstep: 'Well come in. Come in.'

Not long after I was born my father, at Theresa's behest, borrowed some money from his parents in order to buy this house. Hitherto, we had lived in a flat in Shepherd's Bush. And even though I don't suppose Dad much minds where he lives so long as the roof doesn't leak, even though – at the time – he was hard pressed to meet the mortgage repayments on a lecturer's salary, and, with just the three of us, had no use for a four-bedroom house, after my mother left he stayed put – as if unable to relinquish the pitiful hope that one day she'd come back.

'What's this?' he says, as if surprised, when I hand him his present.

'As if you can't guess.'

Opening his card, he remarks of Botticelli's 'Birth of Venus', 'Pretty.' Then, unwrapping his present: 'Oh, a tie! Terrific. Thanks very much.' As, with affected jollity, he tries it on – a brightly patterned affair from Hermès that clashes with both his cardigan and shirt – I belatedly realise that he'll never wear it, that, like everything else in our relationship, it is a sham, and that I'd have done better had I bought him something purely functional – some more batteries, a new tea towel, a pair of underpants. 'What do you think?' he says, turning down his collar.

'Splendid,' I say.

'Really?'

'No. It really suits you.' Then, reassuringly: 'It looks good.'

'Thank you. Thank you, Matthew.'

'My pleasure.'

'Now, what can I get you to drink? Squash? Lime? Bitter lemon?'

'I'll have a Scotch, if that's okay. No ice.'

'Yes, I keep forgetting, you're quite a young man now.'

'I'm twenty-two.'

'Yes. Of course.' Then: 'Anyway. I'll get the drinks. Say hello to your sister.'

I find Sarah in the front room, staring out of the large bay windows at passing cars – or, possibly, at the scuttering sparrow on the front lawn. Sneaking up on her, I blow a noisy raspberry on her cheek and dig my fingers into her left – non-paralysed – flank. Sarah screams with delight.

'Try not to overexcite her,' calls my father from the kitchen.

'Hello, baby,' I say, squatting down beside her, and, with my handkerchief, mopping up her drool.

'Ma–ooh,' she says, thrashing around in her wheelchair. 'Ma . . . uh. – Sruh.'

'Calm down, darling. Here –' removing a bag of sweets from my pocket – 'have one of these.' When I pop the toffee in her mouth, she spits it out in an attempt to speak. '*Ssh*,' I say, popping it back in, running my fingers through her unkempt hair. 'I've missed you too.'

'How does she look to you?' asks my father, handing me my drink.

Sarah is trying to angle her nose on to one of her clawlike fingers. 'Good. Fine. Healthy.' *Fucked*, I think.

'You know, I think she's missed you.'

'I miss her,' I say, abruptly wanting to cry.

'So' – motioning for me to sit – 'how've you been?'

'Fine,' I say, taking a seat on the settee opposite. Then: 'How . . . are you?'

'Oh, I'm . . . fine.' Then, after a pause: 'How's your gran?'

'Oh, you know, same as ever.' I had intended to recount her touching incredulity on the subject of Sapphism. However, in the deepening silence, it suddenly seems hopelessly inapt. I say: 'You're not drinking.'

'No . . . Never been much of a drinker.'

'No.'

'Now my father . . .'

'Yes.'

'He liked a drink.'

'Yes.'

'He drank whisky. Yes. Whisky.'

'Whisky. Yes. I know.'

'Well,' he says finally, 'I'd better check on the lunch.'

My father, to his credit, is an excellent if unadventurous cook. The Yorkshire pudding, when it arrives, is reproachlessly fluffy and light; the roast potatoes crisp and golden; the carrots steamed; the Savoy cabbage chopped and stir-fried in lemon and salt. However, as is his habit, the joint itself is overcooked − or, at least, insufficiently bloody for those carnivores who like their beef more or less raw. In his middle years, Dad, once so dashing and athletic, has put on weight; which isn't to say that he is fat − no, his pot, such as it is, is entirely in keeping with his age and the sedentary nature of his job − and, moreover, obesity demands a capacity for self-indulgence, a lack of restraint, that, in my father, is unthinkable. Indeed, the reason why it's impossible to buy him an apposite present is that the material world, with all its motley pleasures and vices, holds so little fascination for him: he scarcely drinks, he doesn't smoke, he eats in moderation − in short, he doesn't consume. As for his interests, aside from maths and Sarah − and, possibly, me − he doesn't have any. Or at least none that I can discern. Aren't dads meant to be interested in gardening, numismatics, DIY? After Theresa left, as far as I know, he never courted another woman; and all the wretched, unrequited love he felt for his wife he transferred on to Sarah – who, he knew, would always love him and, trapped in her wheelchair, would never leave.

During lunch our conversation degenerates from the phatic ('How's work?' 'Work's . . . fine.') to the tedious ('Super joint. Where did you get it?' 'Oh, you know, the usual place.' 'What – the butchers in the lane?' 'Yes. The butchers. In the lane.') to the taciturn request ('Pass the horseradish, please.' 'Oh yes. The horseradish. Here.'). Why is it that I can effortlessly shoot the breeze with Steve and Clare and Patricia and Kay – with almost anyone at work – but, for the life of me, I'm unable to sustain a conversation with my father for more than a minute?

Finally, he gets around to the subject that I know he's been dying to broach from the moment I arrived.

'So,' he says, staring at his plate, 'your mother called.'

'I saw her last week.'

'How' – attempting to sound off-hand, unconcerned – 'how is she?'

I'd tell him she's divorced but I don't want to get his hopes up. 'She's, um . . . fine.'

'She didn't . . . I don't suppose she . . . well, mentioned me?'

What to say? *Yeah, she said you were shit in bed.* 'No. She didn't.'

He closes his eyes. I can't believe he's still hurt by her indifference. Then, turning to Sarah (who, at the age of eighteen, still needs to wear a bib), he spoons a piece of chopped-up meat and gravy into her mouth. Why is it that I feel more like his father than his son? I want to tell him to let go. To give it up. To find himself another woman. *She's never*

131

coming back. I can't stand feeling sorry for him. Fathers shouldn't inspire pity – they should be upright, resolute, strong! If he'd been a real man she wouldn't have left him. However, watching him with saintlike patience feeding Sarah, I cannot help but love him.

'She's beautiful, isn't she?' he says, wiping some mashed-up carrot from her mouth with the back of his tie – Sarah, who, even in an able body, would've been plain.

'Yes,' I say. 'She is.'

41

To while away the leaden hours after lunch, bound by convention to linger when all we both want is for me to leave, Dad sets up the projector in the drawing-room and shows me some old slides. The first batch were taken on their honeymoon in Paris. The hackneyed snapshots of the sights are in themselves unremarkable – the Eiffel Tower, the Champs Elysées, the Tuileries Gardens, Sacre Coeur. What's fascinating is the foreground, Theresa and Dad, aged, respectively, nineteen and twenty-five. Looking at my father as he was then, only three years older than me, I am struck by the similarities between us. His buoyant brown hair, the cut of his jaw, even small things such as his stance and his patchy stubble are all but identical to mine. As for Theresa, I suddenly comprehend the tenacity of my father's infatuation with her – she is, quite simply, one of the loveliest women

I've ever seen. At once girlish and womanly, feisty, shy –
with her tumbling strawberry-blonde tresses, her peachlike
complexion, her svelte gymnast's frame. It's all I can do not
to caress the projection screen.

The second batch are of me as a baby – looking, I must say,
thoroughly bewildered. In my cot, having my nappy
changed, in the crook of Dad's arm, my expression is one of
persistent puzzlement. Only Theresa, it seems, can make me
smile – slung over her shoulder, kissing me, my dimpled fist
furled around her little finger. I feel I should feel some affinity
with my former six-week-old self – but I don't. I cannot
believe that he is me. Nor discern in his fat man's face my
twenty-two-year-old physiognomy. The carousel whirrs; the
screen goes blank; the next slide appears. I experience a shock
of recognition – I have seen this photo before. I have seen
this photo at Iseult's. It is of Iseult. And me. Yes, he – the
baby whose welfare and whereabouts had so engaged me at
the time – turns out to be me.

'Who's that?' I ask, a little too urgently.

'She's, ah . . . a friend of your mother's.'

'What's her name?'

'I . . . I forget now. Long time ago. I think she and your
mother fell out.' Then: 'Why do you ask?'

'Oh, no reason really. It's just she reminds me of someone
at work.'

'I see.' Then: 'You don't suppose . . .'

'No. She's only twenty. That is, the girl at work. And,
well, that photo's more than twenty years old. So you see,' I
add unnecessarily, 'it can't be her.'

My father looks at me quizzically. 'Evidently,' he says and, turning back to the screen, calls forth the next slide.

42

By the time I arrive at Iseult's it is half past five.

'Mark?' she says into the intercom.

'No. Iseult. It's me.'

'Naughty Boy?'

'Whatever.'

She buzzes me in. Opening the door to her studio, she says: 'Naughty Boy. What a pleasant surprise. Come, let's find you a nappy, shall we?'

Over her shoulder I see that Iseult has been drawing: her plan-chest is strewn with pastels, her easel hastily shrouded with a sheet. Ignoring her, I walk to the kitchen nook, and open the sideboard drawer.

'Naughty Boy! Come back! Where're you going?'

'Shut up.' Then, handing her the pictures: 'Whose are these? Who's *that?*'

Grabbing her riding crop, Iseult makes to silence me with a blow to the head; I deflect the blow with my forearm, and push her to the floor.

'Naughty Boy,' she gasps.

'Fuck Naughty Boy. There is no "Naughty Boy". There's only me.' And, as if to illustrate my point, I smash her riding crop over my knee, and fling the pieces on the floor. 'Now, how d'you know Theresa?'

'Theresa who?'

'Theresa my fucking mother, that's who?'

'You mean you don't know?' says Iseult, smiling ironically, still sprawled on the floor.

'My father said you were friends.'

'He would.' Standing up, 'It's no surprise Theresa left him.'

'Shut up. That's none of your business. Now who the fuck are you?'

'You want a drink?' says Iseult, with infuriating sang-froid, taking a frosted bottle of Stolychnia from the fridge.

'Whatever. I asked you a question. Who –'

'I'm your *aunt*. Theresa's sister. Auntie Iseult.'

'She doesn't have a sister,' I say, docilely accepting my drink.

'Oh but she does,' lighting a Silk Cut.

'Well then why didn't she mention you? Why didn't *you* mention it to *me*? I mean, Christ – I'm . . . No. It's bullshit. You're nothing like her. You don't even *look* like her.'

'I didn't say we were twins.' Then: 'Theresa never told you because . . .' she picks up her vodka, then, changing her mind, sets it on the sideboard. 'She never told you because a long time ago when I was seventeen years old, I . . . borrowed you.'

'You *borrowed* me?'

'Okay. I abducted you. Big difference.'

'You . . . *Why?*'

'I was obsessed with you. Like most adolescents I was terribly needy. Insecure. Bulimic. You understand, I'm not trying to excuse myself. Just . . . Anyway, I'd convinced myself that Theresa was a bad mother – at least I was right about that – and that the only person who really loved you and would look after you properly was, well, me.'

'So you *abducted* me?'

'Theresa and Eric were visiting my parents in Staines. It was the summer holidays. I had some money saved. I didn't really plan it, it just . . . happened. I'd taken you out for a walk – well, you were in your pushchair – we were near the station. And . . . before I knew it, we were boarding a train. At the time it seemed . . . inevitable. Destined. Anyway, the police caught up with me two weeks later in a boarding house in Brighton. Awful place. It was your damn screaming that gave us away. Of course, you missed your mother. I was in a terrible state. I spent the best part of a year in a psychiatric hospital. It was there that I started to paint. Thank God for occupational therapy. Then when I got out I took a foundation course, and applied to the Slade.'

'I . . . I can't believe this. I don't remember.'

'Miff, you were two years old.'

'But surely, I . . .' Iseult refills my empty glass. Then: 'When you . . . you didn't . . .'

'Abuse you? No. Believe me, it was purely platonic.'

'*Platonic?* How can you joke about this? – you crooked bitch.'

'Ouch.' Then: 'Would you like to see what I'm working on?'

When I don't reply, she walks over to her easel and pulls back the sheet. It is a picture of Iseult and me as a baby; we are holding on to one another for dear life: fingers meshed, our arms outstretched, we are being driven apart by some unseen, elemental force. Our bodies extend horizontally in different directions, as if being pulled to opposite ends of a longitudinal abyss. It is a study in loss, the wrenching anguish of separation. I am now standing a few feet from the easel; irresistibly, my hand reaches out for the board.

'You see,' says Iseult standing next to me. 'I've never got over you. Not really. I must've done a thousand variations on the same theme. In a way, it was almost a relief painting your alphabet pictures. I can't tell you what it costs me –' indicating the board – 'to do these.'

'I suppose I should feel flattered. But . . .' All of a sudden I'm struck by the terrible outrage of our incest. 'How could you *sleep* with me, Iseult? How could you fuck me when you knew that I was your nephew? That you were my aunt?'

'Because I thought it would help. Because it seemed like Fate when you started working at The Book Shop and I thought that if I fucked you I might finally break free of this fucking vicious, vicious circle of obsession – but I can't!'

Unable to think of anything to say, I say: 'Who's Mark?'

'My husband.'

'You're *married?*'

'How else could I afford a studio like this?'

'I didn't . . . What does he do?'

'What does it matter?'

'Christ, do you have any kids?'

'No.' Then, staring out of the large dormer window to her right: 'I'm barren.' Then: '*God*, when I think of all the men I fucked trying to get pregnant. Then I met Mark. He was my gynaecologist. He . . .'

'I don't want to know.' Then: 'Look, I think I'd better go.'

'Will I see you again?'

'I don't think so.'

Turning around, she says, all but inaudibly: 'Please don't go.'

'What? You think we can carry on as if nothing happened?'

'I don't know. We could . . . we could go away.'

'To a boarding house in Brighton?'

'Yes. No. I don't know.'

'You need help, Iseult.'

'I *had* help. It didn't help.'

'I'm sorry. But . . . I'm not the answer.'

'Yes,' bitterly, 'it's not your problem. I understand.' Then, as I turn to go: 'I'm sorry.'

'What d'you want me to say, Iseult? That I forgive you?'

'No. I don't want that.' Then, looking out of the window: 'I'm not sorry at all.'

43

Out in the street, I flag a taxi, and give the driver Clare's address. At least, I think, I'm not related to Clare. With Clare I know where I am. We'll drink whisky and smoke dope and have sex – hell, she can even wear Steve's underpants if she wants to, I no longer care. And despite the fact that I have no respect for her as an 'artist' – notwithstanding the fact that she's still committed to her dreams – and have never found her especially attractive, I'm none the less deeply drawn to her as a human being: indeed, on some profound, preverbal level, I have an unshakable faith in her ability to bear my children – perhaps its something to do with the wideness of her hips, the bigness of her breasts, her solidity and seeming indestructibility. Here, my instincts tell me, is a mate – go forth and procreate. And, in Clare, I sense a similarly instinctual response. So then why does the sight of her naked body so often fill me with disgust? Why, whenever we have sex, do I feel somewhat, ever so slightly, sullied? Why do I feel the need to see her now? Perhaps it's because I've nowhere else to go. Because, in all my short pathetic life, she's one of the few people I've regarded as a friend. And even though everyone at The Book Shop vowed to keep in touch, despite the fact that I once thought of us all as an antic kind of clan, I now see that the only thing we had in common was what we did and where we worked – and that without that bond we'll revert to being strangers.

On the threshold of Clare's flat, I'm about to ring the bell when Kirsty's boyfriend opens the door.

'Hey, guy,' he says, in a quasi-American accent.

'Hello . . . I'm sorry, I don't know your name.'

'What the fuck do you care, man? If I give you my *name*, you could give it to anyone. Let's say you get a parking ticket. Let's say you get *five* parking tickets. Let's say,' he rails, rocking back and forth on the balls of his feet, 'you get a whole *bunch* of parking tickets and get in a fix with the filth. When the cops come to you and ask what you got – what're you gonna do? You're gonna cut yourself a deal. You gonna give 'em *my name.*'

It is only now that I notice his M&M-size pupils. 'And

who the fuck are *you* that you're so important? The Una Bomber?'

'I might be,' he says. Then: 'I'm going out for acid, you want some?'

'I skipped breakfast,' I say, which as I say it sounds like a witty retort, only to another question.

In the living room I'm shocked to see two – to me – total strangers fucking on the floor. What's surreal isn't so much that they're both almost fully dressed, nor that they make no noise – although, admittedly, it is odd – but the fact that their faces are so utterly devoid of affect, indeed, bring to mind the stolid impassivity of a lobotomised lunatic. In the kitchen I find Kirsty drowsily smoking a spliff. Although naked, she makes no attempt to cover her small asymmetrical tits – indeed, ignoring me, dips two fingers into a mantled mug of wine and begins to fondle her left nipple.

'Um. Kirsty,' I say awkwardly. 'Sorry to interrupt, but you haven't seen Clare?'

Kirsty languidly inclines the joint towards her lap. And, looking down, just beneath the table, I see Clare's head clamped between her legs.

'A' right, Miff,' she says affably, looking up.

'*Nooo*,' moans Kirsty, pressing Clare's mouth to her cunt.

'There – you *see*,' I say absurdly. Then, again: 'You see?'

On my way back through the living room I notice that the woman, while still being slowly and dispassionately fucked, has turned her head sideways and is now watching cartoons on the muted TV.

Outside, having sprinted down the stairs, I spot Kirsty's boyfriend doing gas with a wasted-looking tramp, and quickly walk in the opposite direction. By and by I hail a taxi to take me to Kay's. Staring fixedly, for some reason, at the back of the driver's head, I try to imagine what his life must be like. In his early thirties, I surmise that he is married. He and his wife fuck in the missionary position twice a week. They have a couple of boys whom they refer to as terrors. And even though they long ago stopped loving each other – if, that is, they ever did – while they both sometimes wish that they'd never met, they each none the less find it all but impossible to envisage an existence unbound-up with the other. However, if I've learnt anything from literature, it's not to presume in other people a simplicity and straightfor- wardness that doesn't exist in oneself – and yet I find it oddly comforting to do so. Perhaps it's because I desperately want to believe in happy families and ordinary lives – men and women unflecked by divorce and adultery. Because I secretly fancy myself as the kind of guy who comes home from the office, kisses his wife, and plays with his kids. Hell, I'll discuss the weather with the neighbours, join the PTA, buy doilies and antimacassars, play golf with my father-in-law . . . And then what, I wonder, does the driver make of me? Obviously, I've had it easy all my life. I'm on the cusp of a lucrative career in one of the professions – medicine, maybe law. Consequently, I think I'm better than him. My fiancée, being similarly pampered and overprivileged, thinks of England when we fuck. And, being a toff, I cannot take my beer . . . Maybe, just maybe, I'll end up marrying Kay. Why the hell not? She'd make a good wife; an excellent mother. I can see our children now, two adorable plum-cheeked putti, a boy and a girl, raptly listening to Kay's bedtime stories. And so what if their mother doesn't burn like a ninja bitch in bed? Other things, I'd like to believe, are more important. Dammit, I'm talking about responsibility! Maturity! Being a Man! I'll relinquish my dreams of writing and work full-time at The Book Shop. With a First from Cambridge, I could become a solicitor or an accountant or a spy. *Kay*, I'll tell her. *Kay, I can't pretend any longer. I love you. I want to marry you. Come be my wife!*

But when I arrive at her flat and press the buzzer, there's no reply. As I'm about to leave, in despair, I hear a window opening above me. Stepping back from the porch I look up and see Kay. 'Oh, Miff. It's you.'

'Yes, it's me,' I say fatuously. Then: 'Look, I don't suppose I could come in?'

'Oh dear. Um . . .'

'What?'

And only then do I see that she's clad in a duvet. 'It's just . . . I'm busy right now.'

'Miff, man. How's it going?' says Rez, looming topless behind her.

'Um. Fine. I think.' Then: 'How . . . are you?'

'I'm doing good. Real *good*,' he replies, grinning wickedly.

'Oh Rez,' says Kay, flushing with pleasure. 'I suppose we'd better tell him now.'

'Tell me what?'

'Rez and I,' she announces proudly, 'are in *love*.' Unbeknownst to Kay, Rez is frantically disclaiming this statement by shaking his head and pulling lunatic faces. 'We're due to be married. Next year. In the spring.' Then, turning to her betrothed: 'Aren't we, Rez?'

'Damn straight.'

'You're the first to know.'

'Congratulations,' I say. 'I'm sure you'll both be very happy.' Then, semi-desperately: 'Is Liz in?'

'Liz? Oh, you mean Beth. No, she's not.' Then: 'Why?'

'I . . . No reason.'

'Are you all right?'

'I'm fine. Really.' Then, over my shoulder as I walk away: 'You'll have to send me an invitation.'

'We will,' calls Kay. 'I promise.'

44

Back at my gran's I find, of all things, a telegram on the table in the hall. MIFF. AM GOING BACK TO AMERICA. MEET ME NOON TOMORROW. REGENT HOTEL. LOVE THERESA. Even my mother, I gloomily reflect, is leaving me. Of course, I should be used to it by now. I remember when I was ten years old, Theresa had promised me a trip to Melbourne; I was to spend Christmas with her and her second husband, Mick. Come the morning of my flight, just as my father was about to drive me to the airport, as he was loading my suitcase into the boot of the car, Theresa rang and cancelled. As she'd cancelled the Christmas before. And the Easter before that. Something about it not being convenient. She and Mick weren't talking . . . he was going away . . . they were getting a divorce. Whatever. But, as always, she vowed to make it up to me. She never did.

And after a while there came a point where there was nothing that a mother could *do* in order to 'make it up', when my disappointments were just too numerous and crushing, my resentment too great, to atone for or restore.

45

Another profitless night of Scotch and cigarettes. Reproachful dreams. As an undergraduate, I was so cocksure of success, I didn't even entertain the possibility of failure. No, late at night, it was all plaudits, reviews, fawning interviews . . . *Miff – I can call you Miff?* Of course. *Miff, your first novel's just been nominated for the Booker. The critics have compared you to Pynchon and Joyce. Rumour has it that you're seeing Cindy Crawford. How do you feel?* Firstly, for the record, Cindy and I are just good friends. As for the praise – well, of course I'm flattered. But also not a little perplexed. What's important to me, first and foremost, is the work. It's what I do to live. So in a way anything else – praise, dispraise, outrage, approbation – is extraneous. I was talking to Mart [in Amis] the other day and he said the same thing: Write. And that's six hours a day. Seven days a week. 365 days a year. *But you've been heralded as a genius. Doesn't that alter your perception of yourself?* Well, to a certain extent, sure. However . . . etc. etc. How hubristic, how fanciful, appears my ambition now. How pitiful the gap between my talent and my dreams. Even in the realm of the attainable, I have failed to attain – a career, marriage, kids.

Fleetingly, romantically and altogether spinelessly I con-template committing suicide. But I am drunk. And every adolescent knows what it is to flirt with death. And even though I may hate my dreams now, for they throw my life into a relief of failure, I cannot honestly claim to've done them justice. Haven't, at bottom, even begun to reach. Nor to live in the adult world of compromise, ambiguity, and all-too-quotidian dismay.

46

Entering the lobby of the Regent Hotel, I spot Theresa sitting in a sumptuous leather armchair languidly leafing through a copy of *Vogue*. She is wearing a smart – for her somewhat conservative – grey Chanel suit. Her lovely flame-hued hair has been pulled back into a severe, almost schoolmarmish, bun.

'Miff, darling,' she says, rising from her seat with outstretched arms.

'Theresa,' I say, briefly embracing her. 'I thought I'd find you in the bar.'

'Yes, well. I thought we might go for a walk. Do something . . . respectable for a change. You know, behave like a mother and son.'

'You be the son,' I say. 'And I'll be Mum.'

Outside, the sky is sharp and pure, a pale glacial blue. Such is my hangover, everything – the sun, the street, people, parked cars – takes on a harsh preternatural clarity. At

Gloucester Gate we turn into Regent's Park. To our right, there is a playground – plangent tykes run amok on slides and climbing frames under the wary supervision of their mums.

'I don't suppose you ever took me to playgrounds.'

'Dear Miff. What must you think of me? Of course I did.'

'I don't remember them.'

'You were young. God, *I* was young. I was the same age you are now. Although at the time I thought I was terribly grown-up. I was married. I was a mother – a fully-fledged adult. Only . . .'

'What?'

'No one . . . no one tells you what to expect. I suppose I pre*sumed* I'd be ecstatically happy. But I wasn't. I never was.'

'Thanks.'

'Sweetie, it wasn't anything to do with you. It was . . . I thought that's what I wanted. Being a bourgeois and playing happy families. Only I felt trapped. I couldn't accept that this was my life – that this was the *rest* of my life. And that the only thing I had to look forward to was growing old and getting fat. I just wasn't *born* to be a mother. I don't know how *they*' – referring to the playground mums – 'do it. They've obviously been blessed – if that's the word – with something I wasn't.'

Today is Easter Monday. The park is filled with families – if not happy, then at least outwardly content. Vaunting their normality. They have dogs and kites and frisbees. Girls and boys. They go to the zoo. Hold hands. Buy soft drinks. These deathless gods of domesticity. We have by now gained the broad walk, and, just beyond the drinking fountain, tack towards the lake. To our right and left are football pitches peopled with warlike boys. Prideful fathers stand on the sidelines shouting hoarse encouragement – it is one of the few aspects of fatherhood that doesn't appeal. As ever I am nonplussed by the fervour and fanaticism occasioned by this – to me – stultifying sport.

I had intended to say something about Iseult. But what? *Theresa, I had sex with your sister. Coincidence, huh? Actually, it was rather amusing, she called me Naughty Boy, I wore a nappy, she beat me with a riding crop.* Instead, I say:

'So, when're you leaving?'

'Tomorrow night.'

'I see.' Then: 'Why?'

'Bernie's said he'll take me back if I forget about my book.'

'But . . . Bernie's *married.*'

'Not for long. He's getting an annulment.'

'On what grounds?'

'Didi, it turns out she's a transsexual. That's *why* she wouldn't sleep with him until they were married. And there was Bernie thinking she was a *virgin.* Really, it's *too* rich!'

'But why take Bernie back?'

'Because . . . Bernie's dependable. Safe.'

'*Dependable?* He *divorced* you.'

'Because, for all his faults, Bernie is rich.'

'But *you're* rich.'

'Am I?'

'*Yes,* you *are.*'

'Dear Miff, I know three million dollars probably *sounds* like a lot of money, but I assure you, it's nothing.'

'But it's *not* nothing.'

'My bill at the Regent's three thousand pounds a week.'

147

'Three *thousand?*'

'Bar bill, laundry, room service – it all adds up.'

'But you don't *have* to live in hotels. You could – we could – we could go away. Where no one knows us. There's nothing keeping me here. We could get a villa in Spain. *Any*where – Monaco, Paris, Milan – I don't care.'

'It wouldn't work,' she says quietly.

'Why *not?*'

'Because I'm your mother.'

'Oh *pah*lease. When have you *ever* been my mother?'

'I'm trying to be one now.'

'Well let me tell you something, *Mum*, it takes a lot more than dressing respectably and wearing your hair in a goddamn bun to cut the mustard as a mother!'

'And besides' – she continues, ignoring me – 'we couldn't possibly *live* off three million. Or at least I couldn't.'

'And that's all that counts?'

'Yes.'

'What about love?'

'What about it? You think love's the key to happiness? Well it's not. And I should know. Love's got *nothing* to do with reality.'

'Well what is the key – money?'

'Of course not. But in the absence of happiness and love – it's all there is. If you'd ever been poor you'd appreciate it. When I was a girl –'

'Yes, yes. You were ashamed of your father because he drove a taxi and your mother because she was working class. My heart *bleeds.*'

'It's a shame you'll never know.'

'Oh really? What about the shame of having a spastic for a sister – and a high society *slut* instead of a mum.'

She turns away. We have come to rest by the foot of the lake. Beyond the railings, two swans eye us imperiously. The honking of geese. The skittering of wings. Waddling ducklings. Finally, she says:

'You'll never know how much I love you.'

'No' – spinning her around to face me – '*you'll* never know how much *I* love *you*. Haven't I been a good son? Haven't I? A scholarship to St Paul's and Cambridge. A fucking First. I mean isn't *that* what mothers want for their sons?'

'I'm very proud of you,' she says, trying not to cry.

'Well why didn't you *say* so?'

'I sent you a case of champagne for your graduation.'

'But I didn't *want* champagne. I wanted you.'

'You think I've had it easy, don't you?' says Theresa, lighting a cigarette.

'Yes. I do.'

'Well I haven't. And don't think for a moment that I haven't felt guilty, because I have – I *do*.'

'Oh, and that makes everything okay, is that it?'

'*Oh*, this is useless.' Staring off at the creamy neo-classical buildings that corral the park, Theresa appears – to me – mythically beautiful, like one of Renoir's blushy river nymphs. 'Do you hate me, Miff?' she says, almost wistfully.

'I thought I did,' I reply. 'God knows, I tried. But however atrociously you treated me . . .'

She turns to face me. 'Yes, darling?'

'You were still my mother.'

'Yes,' kissing me on the forehead. 'I was.'

'You are.'

'I am.'

47

Walking along the Old Brompton Road I run into Anthony.

'Anthony,' I say, unaccountably moved by the sight of him.

'Oh. Hullo, Miff,' he says despondently.

'What's wrong?'

'Nothing.'

But his unkempt appearance – shirt-tails untucked, greasy hair, an unlaced trainer – is eloquent of woe. 'Come on. You can tell me.'

'*Oh*, I feel ridiculous.'

'Why?'

'Miss Collins is getting married to Mr Staunton – the PE teacher. They announced it in assembly on Thursday. I thought I was going to be sick.'

'What say' – my heart quickened by compassion – 'I buy you a drink?'

'Where?'

'The Drayton Arms.'

'But I'm underage.'

'It doesn't matter. I go there all the time. Believe me, they'll serve you. They'll serve me.'

'But . . .'

'What?'

'I'm all spotty.'

'No you're not.'

'That's *why* she doesn't love me.'

'Really, they're hardly noticeable.'

'*Oh*, that's what everyone says. "They're hardly notice-able." When what they *really* mean is: Your face looks like a pepperoni pizza.'

'Anthony, believe me, they're not nearly as bad as you think. No one'll notice. Now come on, let's get that drink.'

'Oh, *all* right.'

We take a table in the corner of the saloon bar. A fan spins above our heads. One of the regulars, a dapper old-timer, sits on a stool at the bar reading the *Mail*.

'Now,' turning to Anthony, 'here's ten quid. Get me a pint of Caffrey's – and I suggest you do the same.'

'But what if they don't serve me?' he asks anxiously.

'Just tell them you're with me.'

As Anthony fearfully approaches the bar I shoot a wink at the barmaid, Rosy, a chesty Kiwi gal who generally stops for a chat when she comes round to collect the glasses and to empty the ashtrays. As she pours the first pint of Caffrey's, Anthony, scarcely able to contain his delight, turns around and gives me a surreptitious thumbs-up. I smile and light a cigarette; feeling, for the first time in months, restful, content. Suddenly I see us as a couple of bachelors. We'll go out on Saturday nights and get regally wrecked. We'll talk about sport and women and cars. In Anthony – who knows? – I may at last have found a male friend. Howbeit, I'm happy for the moment to forget about women – the smoky intimacies and spiky entanglements of sex. Although I can't pretend that the next time I take the tube or go to the cinema or visit a museum I won't keep a look out for my wife. She might even be reading this now. What the hell.

Reader, I'll marry you!